Shadow C...

A Nicholas Chambers Mystery

Christopher J. Dacey

Dedicated to

Nana

ISBN-13: 9781545543368
ISBN-10: 1545543364

Table of Contents

One: Mr. Preston Scott

Preston Scott lived on an expansive Tudor Estate situated in the beachfront town of Charleston, Rhode Island. The estate was secluded and tucked peacefully away in the woods a few miles inland from the Atlantic Ocean. Tall oaks lined the dirt road leading up to the winding driveway at the entrance to the property. I had visited the estate once before, just two weeks earlier when Scott had first called me up to his home.

When I first met Preston Scott, he was standing beside a large flagstone fireplace in the grand ballroom, smoking a pipe and knocking a black iron poker at a pile of red coals smouldering in the large hearth. He was a tall slender man with narrow shoulders, a weak jawline, and dressed in a Harris tweed dinner jacket. His gray hair had a natural wave, and he had a fine trimmed Error Flynn moustache. More than anything else he looked like money to me. That kind of third-generation spoiled money. The type that never had to work very hard for anything, and generally got everything they asked for.

He was looking nervous when I arrived. His wife Elizabeth had reportedly disappeared from the estate without notice a few days earlier. Scott wanted to hire me to track her down. He admitted they had been having the usual troubles and had fought with her the night before she went missing. It was the type of case I generally wanted nothing to do with. More so than not the spouse who went missing wasn't looking to be found. I turned him down at first, but he offered to double my normal rate if I could locate her and bring her back home to him.

I found her a week later in a seedy Providence hotel, shacked up with a much younger man. He was a two-bit insurance salesman named Barnes. The two had apparently fallen hard for one another and decided to run off together. They had made it as far as downtown Providence when the bankroll ran out. By the time I caught up with them the initial gleam of their new relationship had begun to wane, and she was ready to reconcile with her wealthy husband. I put her in a cab and sent her back to the Scott Estate, over the strong objections of her young lover.

That was two nights ago on Friday evening. Scott called me Saturday morning to thank me for finding her and getting her home safely. He asked me to drop by the estate on Sunday evening sometime after eight, to pick up my check and close out the case. By my calculations I had a little over three hundred dollars coming to me.

As I turned down the sloping driveway of the large estate, I noticed the lights in the main building were out. I pulled up to a brick walkway leading to the front door and shut my engine down. As I stepped out of the

DeSoto, I lit a smoke and took a look around. The place seemed dead, silent and enveloped in darkness. There didn't appear to be any lights coming from inside of the main house.

I strolled up the walk to the front doorway and rapped heavy on the brass knocker. I waited for a minute before pounding on it again, but there was still no response. I peeked through one of the side pane windows, but it was too dark inside to see anything. I knocked a third time at the door, as my frustration began to grow. I questioned if I had come by on the right night. When he called me yesterday, I had offered to come by straight away, but he said he had other business to attend to and that I should wait until Sunday evening. I was certain that he had said Sunday evening. I let a few minutes pass as I killed the smoke hanging from my face, finally letting the dead butt drop to the ground.

There was an old rag lying on top of the milk box beside the front door. I picked it up and wrapped it around my knuckles, then punched in one of the glass window panes aside of the door. I reached inside, unlatched the lock, turned the knob and pushed the heavy door open. As I stepped inside, I let my eyes adjust to the darkness.

I was standing in the front foyer of the home. Beams of moonlight from outside pierced through the pane windows, providing a little light to navigate by. In the darkness I could make out the silhouette of the grand staircase at the center of the foyer. It rose to an open platform halfway up, then split off in opposite directions to the second floor. I squinted around the darkened interior and felt something was off. There was a chesterfield with two sitting chairs situated off to the right. I could hear the ticking of the old grandfather clock I had noticed on my first visit, but in the darkness something seemed different.

I reached into my overcoat pocket and pulled out a small pen light that I carried around. I switched the light on and panned it around the place. I didn't like what I saw. The two chairs and sofa were covered with large white sheets. I turned and pointed the narrow beam at the grandfather clock, which was also draped in a heavy sheet.

"Scott?" I called out. No one responded.

I searched the first floor and found that most of the home's furniture had either been removed or covered up. The two large refrigerators in the kitchen had been emptied, and the pantry cabinets were bare. I walked upstairs and found the master bedroom. There were two tall dressers, both empty, and a large walk-in closet with mostly empty coat hangers. Scott along with his wife, had apparently cleared out. Just as I was about to leave the bedroom, I noticed a small tag lying on the polished oak floor. I stooped down, picked it up and put my light on it. It was a small luggage tag that read;

Mr. & Mrs. Preston Scott
C/O Excelsior Hotel
Buenos Aires, Argentina

I tucked the tag away in my pocket. Scott had apparently reconciled and taken his wife on an impromptu holiday. By the looks of the place they weren't planning on returning anytime soon, but more importantly, he had left without paying his bill for my services. Now I knew what the other business was that he needed to take care of.

I went back downstairs and searched the first floor for the envelope I knew he hadn't left for me. I walked back outside and lit another smoke, then got in my car and drove away.

Two: A Bad Monday

My mind was still brooding about Scott when I woke the following morning. It wasn't the first time I had been stiffed by a client, but it never sat well with me. When I got into the office, I'd ask Bridgette to type up a bill for my services and mail it to the Excelsior Hotel in Buenos Aires, Argentina. If I was lucky, it was only an absent-minded oversight on Scott's part, and a check would arrive within the next week or two. But I had been in the business long enough not to put any real hope in that type of thing. I had dealt with rich clients before, and knew they were sometimes difficult to please, and even more stingy with their check books. But sooner or later I would get paid.

I showered, changed, then went into the kitchen to make a fresh pot of coffee and a few eggs. I had just sat down at the table when the telephone rang. The Westinghouse clock on the wall said it was a few minutes past nine. I lifted the receiver.

"Hello," I answered.

"It's me Nick," a female voice spoke over the line. I recognized the soft voice of my secretary Bridgette Hendricks. "He's been here for over an hour already," she explained. "You've got to get down here right away Nick. I can't get rid of him, and there's something about this guy that gives me the creeps," she whispered over the line.

"What guy?" I asked, shovelling a spoonful of eggs in my mouth.

"He said his name is Isaac something or other," she whispered. "This one's a queer bird Nick. Says he needs to talk to you directly and won't say anything else. He's waiting out in the reception area now. I came into your office to make this call," she explained in a hushed voice.

"What does he look like?" I questioned.

"He's in his fifties, short with greasy black hair, and a queer moustache. He's walking with a cane and talks with a foreign accent of some sort, one that I've never heard before.

"Sounds like a lost cause. Tell him to beat it," I suggested.

"I already tried that Nick, but he won't budge. He sat down in that chair and says he'll wait here all day if he has to."

"He'll budge when I get down there," I shot back. "Alright... Tell him to cool his heels and I'll be there within the hour," I relented.

"Ok Nick, just make it quick. I don't the like the way he's looking at me. This one really creeps me out," she said as she hung up the phone. I took a sip of coffee and looked down at my plate of eggs and toast.

"Shit," I said to myself as I got up and tossed the food in the garbage can, then rushed out the door.

Traffic was light on the ride into Providence. The morning sun was cresting over Narragansett Bay as I headed north along Allen's Ave. When I reached the city, I drove along the Providence River. A half-empty trolley passed by, clinging to the tracks on its way up the steep incline of college hill. A policeman directing traffic in front of Union Station held me up for twenty minutes as we waited for a milk truck to clean some broken bottles that had spilled onto the road.

It was a little after ten o'clock when I started up the central stairway of my office building. As I approached the third floor, I could hear men's voices echoing at the far end of the hallway where my office was located. I stepped out onto the polished corridor and saw two uniformed officers standing guard outside of my suite door. One of them put an arm out to me as I approached.

"This area is closed off mister," he informed me.

"This is my office, I'm Nick Chambers," I replied pointing to the name printed in frosted glass on the outer door. The two officers looked dumbfounded at one another.

"One moment Mr. Chambers, I'll need to check with one of the detectives inside," he explained before entering the office and closing the door abruptly behind him.

"What the hell's going on here?" I asked the second officer. He wasn't sure how to answer me.

"There's been an incident inside. You'll have to wait until the detective comes out to speak with you," he explained.

"The hell I will," I replied shoving him down to the ground and busting through the office door. As I entered the reception area, the second officer was already exiting my inner office and rushed at me with his arms out. I landed a heavy right cross on his jaw and he fell hard to the ground. The officer I had left on the floor outside came rushing inside and grabbed me from behind. I reached back, grabbed his shoulder, bent forward and threw him into a small coffee table. He landed hard and the wood splintered under his weight. The officer I had punched was back up on his feet now with his revolver drawn on me.

"Freeze mister!" he shouted. I froze just as the detective inside my office stepped out. It was Tom Bradley.

"Put that gun away Bonin," he ordered the officer. The young officer obeyed the firm command immediately. "What's going on out here Nick?" he shouted at me.

"I was asking the same question, when your boys started playing around with me," I replied. "What in the hell is going on here Tom, and where is Bridgette?" I asked.

"She's inside," he answered. I brushed by him and pushed the door to my office open. The place had been tossed. My desk was on its side and the drawers dumped out on the ground. Books and paperwork from the shelves were sprawled across the oak floor. A couple of scotch bottles that I kept in the cabinet had been broken against the wall. The Davenport had been gutted and its insides pulled out.

The most disturbing sight was lying slumped over the side of my desk chair. Her bare arms hung down loosely, her fingertips scraping at the floor. Her head was tilted up, her beautiful jade eyes still open and staring up at the ceiling. Her throat had been cut and she was very dead. I stood motionless for a moment in a state of unexpected shock. I didn't hear Tom walk inside the office behind me.

"Your secretary?" Tom asked. I nodded unable to speak. "It doesn't help to look at her Nick," he advised as he tugged at my coat. I brushed him off again and knelt down beside her lifeless body. I closed her eyes with one hand and held her cold hand with the other.

"I should have got here sooner," I murmured to myself.

"Do you know anything about this Nick?" he questioned. I shook my head.

"Not really," I replied. "She called me at home an hour ago and said there was a new client down here looking to see me. I told her to have him sit tight and that I would be down as soon as I could."

"What client?" Tom asked.

"I don't know, she only said that it was a man." I replied half-truthfully. I had a first name and a pretty decent description, but I wasn't about to give it to Tom or to the police right now. They could do their own investigation, and I would do mine. I couldn't have the police getting in my way. Whoever he was, he was going to pay. There wouldn't be a plea deal or life sentence for this scumbag. He would pay with his life, and I planned on doing the collecting.

"No description of the man?" Tom probed.

"No," I replied stoically.

"Did he have an appointment Nick?"

"No… She said he just showed up here this morning and insisted on waiting for me," I answered. "She said he gave her the creeps." I added. Just then the door to the office opened and a tall man wearing a white lab coat walked inside. He was carrying a black doctor's bag. Tom recognized him and shook hands.

"She's over there, behind the desk Bill," Tom instructed pointing in my direction. "This is Dr. Bill Walters Nick, the City Coroner. Let's go outside and leave him to his work," he suggested. I let go of

Bridgette's hand and stood up slowly, wiping a single tear from my face, then followed Tom outside.

He handed me a smoke as we walked out into the hallway, passing by the two officers I had wrestled with on the way in. I took my lighter out and lit the cigarette. I noticed my hand was shaking as I put the lighter back in my pocket.

"Working on anything right now Nick?" he asked. I thought about Mr. Preston Scott and his sudden trip to Buenos Aires for a moment but dismissed it as he didn't fit the description Bridgette had given me over the telephone. I shook my head.

"Nothing... It's been damn quiet," I replied while taking a deep drag on the smoke. "I don't have any idea who did this Tom, other than whoever did is in line to be Dr. Walter's next customer." He jerked me around by the shoulder.

"Don't even think about it Nick. You head directly home and slug back a highball or two to calm your nerves. We'll find the guy that did this. I know how you feel, but give us a chance to do our job," he advised. "I'd hate to be locking your sorry mug up if you go and do something stupid," he added.

"Ok pal... I'll go home and have that drink," I answered. "Just let me know if you find anything Tom. I'm owed that much at least." He nodded.

"I'll keep you posted Nick," he answered. "You've got my word on it." I nodded and walked away.

Three: Nick Chambers Investigates

As I stepped outside onto the hot pavement of Westminster Street, I stood there dizzy and motionless, invisible to the pedestrian traffic that blurred by me in both directions.

The events of the morning were racing through my mind. An unknown man by the name of Isaac, assuming that was his real name, had shown up in my office early that morning asking to meet with me and refusing to leave. He had given Bridgette the creeps, which prompted her to call me, or maybe that was his intention? He may have wanted to know how long it would be before I reached the office. He wouldn't want me walking in on his handiwork. Based on Bridgette's description, he was a short man with black hair and a moustache. He spoke with an accent. He was in his fifties and carried a cane. That was all I had... Hell, it would have to be enough.

Whoever he was, he had killed Bridgette and rifled through my office. Whoever he was he had just made a very serious mistake. I took a quick look around on the off chance the scum bag was still lurking somewhere close by. Sometimes these twisted types liked to hang around and watch. I scanned the street and sidewalks, then the buildings and rooftops, but came up empty.

A young newsy was standing on the corner with his canvas bag of morning bulletins. I recognized the kid as Liam O'Rourke. Liam had dropped out of high school about a year ago and got pinched soon after for stealing half a dozen cases of beer from a delivery truck. It landed him in juvenile detention. I knew the family, so I helped him out of the trouble and into a job at the Providence Journal. He seemed to be back on track now. I walked up and tossed a nickel at him.

"Hey there Mr. Chambers," he greeted. I nodded back as he handed a morning edition to me. "How's your day going?" he asked.

"I've had better Liam," I replied. "I could use your help on something." A look of excitement took over his youthful face.

"A case?" he questioned enthusiastically. "Whatever the job is, I'm your man Mr. Chambers." I smiled back at him. He couldn't be more then sixteen years old, but he knew his way around the city and might make a capable operative.

"This is important Liam, I need to know if you saw anyone going in or out of my building this morning. A short man in his fifties, slick black hair with a moustache. He may have been carrying a cane. He would have gone in sometime before nine o'clock, and would have come out sometime over the past hour?" I questioned. Liam rubbed the side of his temple as if to loosen up his memory.

"I wouldn't have seen anyone going in at that time because I was picking up my papers at the Journal Building around nine, and it took me about a half hour to work my way over here," he explained. His forehead scrunched as he thought pensively for a moment. "No, I don't think... Hold on just a second!" he exclaimed. "When I first got over here there was someone getting into a car just in front of your building. It could have been the same guy. In fact, he did have a cane with him! I remember thinking how odd it was."

"Odd in what way Liam?" I asked.

"It was one of those fancy walking canes," he replied. "Black, with a shiny golden handle. The handle was carved into some sort of animal's head. It could have been a lion, but I can't be sure. He got into the back seat of the car and it drove off right away."

"What type of car was it?" I asked anxiously. He rubbed the side of his head again, coaxing the memory out from inside of his skull.

"It was a sedan, a pretty fancy one. Maybe a Packard or a Cadillac. It had a set of new white wall tires," he recounted.

"What year was it?" I asked.

"It had to be a thirty-nine or a forty," he replied.

"Did you see where it was headed?"

"It headed down Westminster Street by the banks, towards the riverfront," he answered. I looked down the road in that direction.

"Thanks Liam!" I said. "Keep an eye out for that car or for the man himself. It's very important. If you see them anywhere, call me right away. My home number is WI-4412. Remember, call me if you see anything," I repeated. He took a half-chewed pencil out from behind his ear and scribbled my number down on a small scratch pad.

"You can count on me Mr. Chambers," he answered.

"Thanks Liam, but there's just one other thing," I added. "If the police come down and question you about anything, you didn't see a thing, including me, that car or the man who got into it. This is too important a case, and I don't need the police getting in my way and mucking things up." He nodded to say that he understood.

"Mums the word Mr. Chambers. I won't say nothing about anything to anyone. I'm your man," he reminded me. I thanked him and walked off in the direction of the Providence River.

The walk down to the waterfront was surreal and half-conscious. I burned a couple of smokes on the way thinking about Bridgette, and the look on her lifeless face. I passed by the Arcade and the financial district, glancing up at the tall Industrial Trust building. I stopped at a lot near the post office and spoke with a friend of mine who parked cars there. No car fitting the description had been there. I turned right onto Dyer Street and began walking aimlessly along the riverfront, passing by the first two piers.

As I approached the Dorrance Street Pier, I noticed a black sedan parked next to a warehouse at the far end of the road, close to the pier. I couldn't make out the model from where I was standing, so I turned and headed along the road towards the water.

I was about half way down when two large mugs in longshoreman's coats and black knit caps stepped onto the road directly in front of me. They were both over six feet in height, broad-shouldered, with square jaws and rough unshaven faces. The one on the right seemed to have one dead eye. I thought to myself that they could have been twins at one time, but life had been hard on both of them and any cuteness had faded long ago. The man on the right was carrying a crowbar and his partner on the left clasped a blackjack in his hand.

"What's your business mister?" the one-eyed man asked.

"No business, just having a walk and a smoke," I answered.

"Go smoke somewhere else," the second thug advised. "This ain't no city park mister," he added. I took a slow drag from my cigarette and thought it over. These two had picked the wrong morning to threaten me. A good fight sounded therapeutic right now. Bridgette was dead, and I needed to take it out on someone. These two jugheads fit the bill as much as anyone would.

"But fellas, I always take my morning stroll down by the river," I said in a puzzled tone. "I generally meet the nicest people in this part of town. Take the two of you... Clearly, two fine upstanding citizens… A couple of intellectuals. I could tell that right off. I said to myself these two seem like stand-up gentleman, pillars of our society. I'm guessing you both teach over at Brown University?" I asked. They looked at each other for a moment. The barb took a moment to prick them.

"Looks like we found ourselves a comedian Mick," the one-eyed man remarked. "Alright soldier, we'll see if you're still cracking wise once I straighten your teeth with this crowbar," he suggested.

"So you fellas are actually dentists? I should have guessed. As much as I could use a good teeth straightening, I don't think I'd have time for it right now. But I've got a molar that's been aching something awful. Maybe I could make an appointment?" I asked.

The one-eyed man's face painted red and he came at me. I closed the gap between us as he lifted the crowbar over his head. He swung it down hard, but I blocked his wrist with my left forearm. The crowbar came loose, bounced off the side of my head and dropped onto the pavement. I swung a heavy right cross at his blind side. It connected hard to the side of his face. He felt the impact and reeled backwards.

I turned just in time to side-step a charge from his twin brother. As he passed by me, I managed to get my leg in front of his, tripping him and sending him sprawling onto the ground. I picked the crow bar up off the street. The man with the black jack recovered quickly and came charging back at me. This time he swung the lead weapon in the direction of my head. I stepped in and struck his forearm with the crowbar, then felt the crack of a bone somewhere under his heavy overcoat. He dropped down to one knee as the blackjack fell from his hand.

A moment later a heavy fist struck my face from the right side. In the excitement, I had lost track of his one-eyed friend. A bell rang hard inside of my skull alerting me of the impending danger. I kept on my feet, but the world was moving in slow motion now. His friend stood up, grasping at his broken arm. He took the black jack from the ground with his good hand and stepped up in front of me. I tried to lift my arms to defend myself, but something was holding them down. Without my realizing, a vice grip had clamped down over them from behind. The man in front of me grinned as he lifted his good arm up above his head. The blackjack came crashing down on top of my skull and the lights went out.

Four: A Long Ride Home

I could smell the fresh sea air passing gently through my nostrils as I slept comfortably on my soft bed. The bed rocked gently as my eyes gradually opened. The morning sky was clear, blue, and dotted with sparse white clouds. The sound of seagulls calling to one another passed in and out of my ears.

As I turned over, the bed I was lying on felt suddenly damp. I lifted my head from the wet surface and took a half-conscious look around. I was lying on an expansive sheet of dirt, shale and clay, the type that had recently been scrapped from riverbeds to make room for passing ships.

I sat up slowly, taking care not to magnify the throbbing sensation going on inside of my skull. I reached back and felt a large egg on my head, and dried blood that had caked up in my hair. I sat there for a few minutes without moving, letting the blood rush back to where it belonged. I looked down at my legs, which were partially sunken beneath the murky surface. I finally worked up the strength to clear the mud off and stand up.

I was standing on top of several tons of dredged river bed from the Port of Providence. The flat barge that carried it was being towed by a tug boat about fifty yards off the bow. We seemed to be heading south out of Narragansett Bay at around five knots. I recognized the waterfront as we passed by the Rhode Island Yacht Club in Cranston, then crouched down instinctually to be sure I was out of the tug boat captain's line of sight. Five minutes later we passed by Pawtuxet Cove, heading in the direction of open ocean. In thirty minutes, we would be out in the Atlantic and my options would be limited. I knew these dredging barges usually went twenty or so miles out into deep water before dumping their loads. I had to swim for it while the shore was still in range.

As we approached Gaspee Point, he began to steer the tug to the port side to avoid the sand bar protruding from the shore. I took my shoes and jacket off, then walked to the edge of the barge. There was a fifteen-foot drop from the edge down to the water's surface. I glanced at the shoreline and saw that it was high tide, then dove in.

The water felt like a sledge hammer on my tender head as I passed beneath its dark surface. I went down about three meters before slowing and swimming back up for air. It was September and the cool water roused me from my slumber. I turned and saw the tug still working hard to pull the heavy barge out to sea.

I started swimming for the shoreline about a hundred yards off, taking my time side-stroking most of the way in. Fifteen minutes later I washed up on the sand bar at Gaspee Point, then laid there for some time like a beached whale. No one in the shanty houses high above on the cliff seemed to notice me. The sun felt good on my swollen face, and I was more out of breath then I had expected to be. When the oxygen finally returned to my lungs, I stood up and began walking barefoot across the sand. When I reached the end of the beach, I walked along a small path that led up a hill to a narrow dirt road. I followed the road about a mile through Brown's Farm, finally reaching the main road.

The trolley coach heading into providence was coming up the road. I checked my pants pocket and pulled a nickel out. The coach came to a stop in front of me and opened its door. I stepped inside and dropped my nickel into the coin slot. The driver gave me a dubious look as I walked past him barefoot and still dripping from my morning swim. I wasn't sure if he noticed the lump on my head or my swollen eye.

"How far mister?" he questioned sceptically.

"Pawtuxet village," I answered, taking the third seat from the front. He pushed the voltage lever forward and the trolley bus began to pull away.

I sat there quietly, damp and dazed from the morning's events. I pulled the split window down and let some fresh air breeze in across my swollen face, then thought about the two thugs I had encountered back on the Pier. The Providence waterfront had a reputation for being a pretty rough area, but coming at me with a crowbar just for walking down the wrong street, and tossing me on a barge for deep sea disposal seemed a little extreme. I wondered if the black sedan I had spotted near the warehouse was the same one Liam had seen leaving my building. I wondered why anyone would kill an innocent young girl like Bridgette. I wondered what the cops were doing with her right now. By this time, she was out of the office and down at the city morgue. I didn't have a lot to go on, other than the quick description she had given me over the telephone, along with Liam's account of a Packard or Cadillac leaving the area. It would have to be enough.

Ten minutes later the bus stopped on Broad Street in Pawtuxet Village to drop me off.

"You ok mister?" the driver questioned as I passed by him on my way out.

"No... I'm not," I answered honestly, before stepping down onto the sidewalk.

He dropped me just over the Pawtuxet River Bridge in front of Cameron's pharmacy. My apartment was about a block away, above Lindsey's Market on the third floor. I went into the pharmacy and picked up a bottle of scotch. The clerk eyeballed the wet dollar bill I handed him, but eventually tucked it away in the register and made change for me.

As soon as I was back outside on the sidewalk, I took a healthy swig from the pint, then headed up to my apartment. As I entered the building, an elderly patron was exiting the market, so I held the door open for her. She nodded thanks but noticed my bare feet and commented.

"Better put some shoes on young man, or you'll catch your death of cold," she advised. She didn't say anything about the scotch bottle in my hand. It was September and seventy degrees out. I just nodded in agreement and headed up the stairs.

When I reached the top, I pulled a spare key from under the front mat, unlocked the door and went inside. It was a small loft apartment, dingy and run down, but it met my needs. The main living room doubled as a bedroom and looked down onto Broad Street. There was a modest kitchenette and bathroom on the opposite side. I undressed, stepped into the shower, and rinsed the sand and salt from my aching body. When I came out, I threw on a fresh pair of jeans and a clean shirt, then poured myself a highball and sat down on the chesterfield.

I threw back most of the scotch and thought about the morning's events. Bridgette was dead, worse off she had been killed inside of my office. She had called me for help, and I had let her down. It was only a matter of time before I was face-to-face with her killer, and when I was it would be payback time. I reached up and felt the tender egg nestled on the back of my skull. If I didn't have enough trouble already, there were two longshoreman I needed to balance the books with. I leaned back on the sofa and let my eyes roll down.

Sometime later, a loud knock on the door woke me. A sat up slowly and noticed that darkness had already settled in outside. The window was half open, and I could hear traffic passing by on the street below. I sat there for a moment alone in the quiet darkness, before a heavy knocking interrupted the peaceful solitude once again.

"Chambers!" a loud voice barked outside in the hallway. I stood up slowly and made my way over to the door.

"Open up shamus!" a second voice ordered. I unlocked the door and pulled it open. Two bulldogs stood ominously outside in the hallway. I recognized the tall man on the right as Detective Tom Bradly. The second man was older and slightly shorter than Tom.

"Tom," I nodded as the two men stepped into the apartment uninvited. I shut the door behind them. "Come right in," I remarked sardonically. They walked into the main room.

"Got a minute Nick?" Tom asked.

"I suppose so," I answered. "Can I get you gents a drink?" I offered.

"Not now Nick," Tom answered. "We've got some questions."

"Alright boys, then have a seat in the parlor while I make myself one," I instructed. I walked into the kitchenette and poured a double scotch into a tall glass, then opened the freezer for an ice cube. What I saw inside sent a shock wave through my body and roused me from any lingering slumber. An unfamiliar object had been placed in the front of the freezer. It was a long curved stainless-steel blade with a gold-plated handle. There was a frozen caked-up dark substance on the blade. I reached over it and pulled the ice cube tray out, then closed the freezer.

When I returned to the parlour both detectives had taken seats in the two easy chairs. I sat down on the Chesterfield with my highball.

"Well boys, what can I do for you?"

"You look like hell Nick? What happened to you today, or do I even what to know?" Tom questioned.

"A couple of mugs down by the dock didn't like the way I looked, so they tried to adjust my face with a tire iron," I explained.

"They're funny that way," Tom commented.

"Exactly where were you this morning around nine o'clock?" The second detective questioned impatiently. Tom turned to the man and shot a frustrated look at him.

"I was here," I answered. "I had just woken up. It was a few minutes after nine when Bridgette called me. But then again, I already told you that this morning. Maybe you fellas need me to write it down for you, so you can remember it next time.

"It's just routine Nick," Tom explained. "We need to eliminate you as a suspect."

"To hell with the two of you!" I shouted back. "Couple of class acts. Coming down here the same night Bridgette gets killed and accusing me."

"Hold on just one second Nick," Tom interrupted.

"What the hell is this all about anyway?" I shouted, standing up abruptly and throwing my glass against the wall. "Why don't you check with the switchboard operator. I'm sure she'll remember the call going out. Maybe if you're lucky she even listened in on it. But that would take some honest detective work." The two men stood up from their chairs.

"Alright Nick… We'll come back in the morning," Tom offered. "He's too tight to answer any questions now Pete," Tom whispered to the second detective. The second detective spoke up.

"We got two witnesses who put you in the building early this morning Chambers, before the girl was killed, and by the way, we did check with the switchboard operator and she doesn't remember any calls going out from your office this morning. That adds up to two things Chambers. First one is that you were in the building at the time the girl was killed, and the second is that you lied to us about being there. We need to search this place Tom," the second detective stated.

"Go ahead!" I shouted angrily. "Search the place all you like. I got nothing to hide from you clowns." Tom reached over and tugged the second detective by the arm.

"Let's go Pete," he ordered. "He's had a rough day. He'll be sobered up by morning. We can come back and talk to him then." The second detective shot a dirty look at me but went grudgingly out the door with Tom.

As soon as they had left, I locked the door and listened for their footsteps to reach the bottom of the stairway. The screen door on the first-floor opened, then slammed shut. I ran back to the freezer and used an oven mit to remove the half-frozen blade, then took a good look at the object under the kitchen light.

It was a straight thin stainless-steel blade, no more than a half inch in width. The blade was approximately six inches in length, razor sharp, and stained in areas with a red frosted substance that most likely was Bridgette's blood. The handle felt heavy and looked to be made of gold, with four red rubies embedded in it. The hilt had a several designs carved on it, along with one unusual symbol that I didn't recognize. It reminded me of a knife I had seen once before, although I had never seen this particular knife.

Someone had taken the time to plant it in my apartment for the police to find. Maybe that same someone had called the police to suggest they should come by and search my place tonight. If it wasn't for my friendship with Tom, they probably would have. They would back the morning, so it had to go.

I had an old newspaper lying on the kitchen table and placed the cold weapon down on top of it. I rolled the knife up inside the funnies and tied it tightly with some string, then wrapped the whole package up in a brown paper bag. I addressed it to Detective Tom Bradley, c/o the Providence Police Station.

I had a few stamps in the drawer and put enough on to do the job. I didn't list a return address. I walked downstairs to Lindsey's Market and dropped the parcel in the outgoing mail slot, headed back upstairs, locked my door and went to sleep.

Five: A New Day

By morning I was done feeling sorry for myself. I got up early, showered, and was out the door before the police arrived to search my place.

I walked down Broad Street and stopped on the Pawtuxet River Bridge to have a smoke. The fog in my head was beginning to clear. I tried to relax, watching the black water pass slowly beneath me. There was something about flowing water and the ocean that always seemed to calm my nerves. Yesterday had been a bad day for the Nick Chambers Detective Agency, especially bad for Bridgette Hendricks, bad for the back of my skull, bad all around.

I looked down at the quaint scene in Pawtuxet Cove. The morning sun was rising on dozens of small boats tied up in their slips. A few tired-looking fishermen were loading up bait and preparing for their day's work. Behind me, I could hear the water raging on the falls side, just before the bridge. But the water emerging beneath me and flowing out into Pawtuxet Cove was almost still and peaceful.

I was raging on the inside yesterday, but a good night's sleep had cleared my head and calmed my anger. I knew that I would need every bit of experience and intuition to work through this case. The second detective last night said they had two witnesses who saw me in the office building early yesterday morning before Bridgette was killed. He also seemed pretty intent on searching my place, which made me think the police had been tipped off by someone. If they had searched the place, it was even money they would have found the knife that had been planted in my freezer. It was hidden away just enough for me not to notice it, but not enough to escape a thorough police search. All of that together would have looked pretty bad for me, and most likely would have landed me in a jail cell for the rest of my life.

Whoever had killed Bridgette had left the building unnoticed, planted a murder weapon in my apartment, phoneyed-up a couple of witnesses to place me on the scene, and had done a pretty fair job convincing the police that I was a suspect. Someone had gone to a lot of trouble to throw suspicion on me and seemed to be setting me up for the fall. I knew I was up against an intelligent and formidable killer. I would need to leave the emotion of Bridgette's death behind for the time being and get down to business.

"It's nice here early in the morning, wouldn't you say?" a voice beside me spoke. I turned to see an old man standing next to me on the bridge and looking down over the cove. It was old man Ingram. He was well into his seventies now, but he had been a police officer for nearly forty years. His beat for most of that time had been walking up and down Main Street in Edgewood and Pawtuxet Village. He had retired a few years back, but old habits die hard with his type.

"How are you Frank?" I greeted. He smiled and looked out over the water, pulled a pipe out and tucked some tobacco inside, then set fire to it.

"My favorite part of the day is watching the sun rising up over the cove. Usually here by myself, but it's always nice to have a little company Nick," he added. I nodded.

"Sorry to crash the party, but I've got a long day ahead and wanted to get an early start on things."

"More detective work?" He questioned.

"Yeah... More detective work," I answered stoically. "I wonder if you could do me a favor Frank? I think someone may have broken into my place yesterday, and there's a chance they might try it again today. Would you mind keeping an eye on the place for me?" A smile erupted across his weathered face.

"Of course I can," he answered. A pilot light deep inside his retired mind ignited suddenly and stoked his interest. "Leave it to me Nick, no one will get near your place. I'll make sure of that," he added.

"Actually Frank, I'm pretty sure whoever broke in yesterday is very dangerous. So better steer clear of any direct confrontations. If you could just keep an eye out from a distance and let me know if anyone goes in or out," I advised.

"Alright Nick," he answered. "But you take all the fun out of it." I smiled back at him.

"There's nothing in there that I care that much about. But I could sure use a good description and a license plate number if you can manage it."

"If anyone shows up, you'll have both," he reassured me. I shook his hand in thanks and walked away.

"Oh yeah," I added turning back. "The police should be by sometime this morning, but they're not who I'm worried about."

"So... It's that way is it?" he questioned. I nodded grudgingly.

"It's that way alright," I replied. I turned and walked off.

I stopped inside the drug store and bought a pack of smokes, then sat down at the lunch counter for a cup of coffee. When I had finished, the cashier called a cab for me, which arrived about ten minutes later. I told the driver to take me downtown, to the spot I had left my car the day before. He drove me there without much conversation and dropped me in front of the lot. I paid him and walked up to the shanty guard shack. A short pudgy man stepped out from inside and waved at me. Eddy Preston was the day guard at the lot.

"It's about time you showed up Nick. I was starting to worry about you. You never leave it here over night. The boss was telling me this morning I should have it towed," he reported.

"Did you?" I asked.

"Nothing doing," he replied. "I told him you're a good customer and you'd be by sooner or later for it," he explained.

"Thanks Eddy," I replied gratefully.

"Of course, when the police came by yesterday, I had to let them search it," he added.

"The police were here?"

"Just before rush hour," he explained. "They asked to search your car, and they asked in a way that didn't leave much room for discussion."

"They find anything?" I questioned.

"Yeah... They found that thirty-eight you keep tucked under the dash."

"Was that it?" I probed.

"Yeah, that was all they found. I watched them the entire time, told them I was responsible for all the vehicles parked here, and I needed to be sure they didn't damage anything," he reported.

"They must have loved that," I replied. He laughed.

"The two cops who searched it seemed pretty annoyed with me, but I don't give a crap. I got my rights too, I told them. I need to look out for my customers vehicles," he added tilting his head in my direction. I got the point and pulled a couple of bills out from my wallet and handed them to him.

"Thanks Eddy! Got my keys?" I asked. A troubled expression painted his face as he sunk his head in shame.

"Sorry Nick... Those coppers took your keys and said I should give them a call if you showed up here for the car," he explained.

"How about popping the ignition for me Eddy?" I asked. "I've got some work to do today, and I need wheels."

He nodded and walked back into his shack, re-emerging a minute later with a screwdriver in hand. We walked over to my coupe and he slid behind the wheel, then went to work on the ignition. After a minute or two of effort, I heard a metallic pop inside. Eddy stepped out from the car and handed the ignition to me, along with the small screwdriver. "Keep it to use as a key Nick," he instructed.

I thanked him and slid behind the wheel. I put the screwdriver into the small exposed slot, and turned it. The engine roared to life. I tossed the driver on the front seat beside me and drove away.

Six: An Unlikely Lead

I headed a few blocks down Westminster Street, back in the direction of the waterfront. I wanted to canvass the area on the off chance of spotting the black sedan Liam had seen. The Providence River was dark and still under a clouded sky. I drove along the riverfront for over an hour but came up empty, then crossed over to the east side and ran laps up and down college hill. I even drove down the same narrow alleyway by the river where I had met the two goons a day earlier. This time I had a crowbar of my own on the front seat in case they wanted to come out and play with me again, but the area seemed completely deserted today.

I drove to the end of the road, to the small warehouse where I had noticed the black sedan parked a day earlier. I parked the DeSoto out front and took a walk around the building. The side doors were locked, and two heavy steel garage doors out back had been padlocked. I peered through a set of grimy windows, but the place seemed empty inside. I was just about to go back for the crowbar to help pry a window open, when I noticed a small fishing trawler pulling up to the dock behind the warehouse. I got in my car and drove back into the city.

As I passed in front of Union Station, I noticed a familiar figure standing on the street corner. The young man waived me down as I approached. I pulled up to the curb and rolled the passenger side window down.

"What's up Liam?" I asked.

"I saw that Packard again Mr. Chambers," he reported proudly. I pulled up on the curb and shifted the car into park.

"When?" I asked anxiously.

"Last night," he answered. "I was out selling the Evening Bulletin, about two blocks away over near City Hall. It pulled up to the curb and the driver got out to buy a paper from me. I recognized the car right away. It was a Packard for sure. Got a good look at it this time," he added.

"Did you get a plate number?"

"You told me to, didn't you," he answered enthusiastically, before pulling a small scrap of paper out from his receipt book. "Here you go," he offered as he handed the folded paper over to me.

I unfolded the scrap and read what he had scribbled down in pencil;

> *19   Washington DC   40*
> *Foreign   314*
> *Gov't*

"This was the license plate?" I asked.

"You bet! I pulled my pencil out and wrote it down when he was getting back into the car," he explained. "It wasn't a Rhode Island Plate, so I figured you'd want me to write everything down. It was yellow with black letters."

"Are you sure it was the same car?" I questioned. He nodded.

"I'm sure," he asserted. "Don't see a fancy car like that around here every day. All that chromium in the grill, and those Packard hub caps on the tires." he added.

"What did the driver look like?" I asked

"He was tall, about your height, dressed in one of those brown chauffeur outfits. He looked about twenty-five, had short dark hair and wore a drivers cap."

"Anything else kid?" I asked. Disappointment rolled down his face. He was clearly expecting more of a reaction from me, but I was still too numb to give him the reaction he was looking for.

"As a matter of fact, there was a couple of other things," he stated with indignant pride.

"Don't keep me in suspense," I prodded.

"When he took his wallet out to pay me, he dropped a card on the ground. I picked it up and handed it back to him. It looked like some type of membership card."

"Membership to where?"

"The Turks Head Club," he replied. "That's up in the Turks Head Building, right?"

"Yeah," I answered.

"There was one last thing," he added. "I noticed a parking permit inside of the front windshield."

"Permit to where?"

"Chateau something or other. I couldn't read the whole thing before the car drove away."

"Was the man with the cane in the car?"

"No," he answered. "He wasn't in the car, it was just the driver." I pulled a fin out from my wallet and handed it to him.

"Nice job kid! You'd make a pretty fair detective," I complimented. A smile took back control of his face.

"Five bucks!" he said, examining the bill as if it were counterfeit.

"You'll still need earn some of that dough kid," I added.

"I'll earn it," he replied tucking the bill away in his pocket. "Whatever you need, I'm your man!"

"You've been up to my office before?" I asked. He looked over his shoulder and nodded his head.

"It's up on the third floor of the Burrows Block Building, right?" he asked.

"That's right," I replied. "Here's the key to my suite. I need you to head up there pronto and bring something back down here to me. If I go up there myself the cops will tie me up with endless questions, and I can't afford to get hung up with them right now. I'm guessing they have a man in the downstairs lobby waiting on me. If he stops you just say you've got your deliveries to make," I advised.

"Sure thing Mr. Chambers," he replied. "I'll be back in a flash. You can count on me!" He gushed enthusiastically. "What do you need me to get?"

"On the right side of my desk, there's a forty-five taped under the bottom drawer. Pull the whole drawer out and you'll see it. Drop it in your newspaper bag and come back down." I instructed. Liam's eye's bugged out.

"A gun?" he questioned.

"The police already took the gun I keep in my car, so I need my back-up," I explained casually. He nodded slowly to register his understanding of the situation. "You've handled guns before, right kid?"

"Of course I have," he stated indignantly.

"Well then get going and meet me back here in ten minutes. If there's anyone up in that office, forget the whole deal and come right back down. I've got a phone call to make in the meantime." He nodded hesitantly and ran off.

I pulled the DeSoto up on the curb beside a telephone booth, then left the engine running while I stepped outside to make a quick call. I dropped a nickel in the coin slot and dialed. The telephone rang twice before the switchboard operator lifted the receiver on the other end.

"Providence Police Department, how may I help you?" a female voice greeted.

"Detective Tom Bradley," I requested.

"One moment Sir." The phone rang three times before Tom's deep voice echoed across the copper line.

"Detective Bradley," he barked. I could tell by the harsh tone that he wasn't having a good morning.

"It's Nick Tom," I said. I heard a heavy exhale of exasperation on the other side of the line.

"Where in the hell are you Nick?" he questioned. "The boys are down searching your place right now," he added.

"I figured as much. I left to give them some time to go through the place. I wouldn't be able to sit there while they toss my stuff Tom."

"Well, just get your sorry ass down to the Precinct," he ordered.

"I'll be down soon enough," I answered. "What's this about two eye witnesses seeing me in the building early yesterday morning. That's a bunch of hooey Tom." I could feel his frustration seeping across the line.

"Well get down here and tell that to the Lieutenant Nick," he shouted. "There were two witnesses. The first was some old biddy selling flowers out in front of your building. She said she sees you on your way in every morning, and that you usually stop to say hello, sometimes you even buy a flower from her. She said she was surprised to see you there so early yesterday, and that you seemed distracted, walked right by her without saying hello. The second witness was a delivery man dropping off a package on the third floor. His name is Sampson. He said he saw you going up in the elevator just before nine o'clock."

"I never met either of them, and if you question the regulars in the building they'll tell you the same. I'm not sure what's going on here Tom, but it looks like someone is going through a lot of trouble to set me up as a fall guy."

"What makes you say that?" he asked.

"You'll be getting a parcel in the mail later today. A little item I found tucked away in my freezer when I got home last night. I didn't want your boys finding it in my place," I explained.

"Murder weapon?" he questioned.

"Looked that way to me," I replied.

"That looks bad Nick. I don't see how mailing it to me help matters?"

"I thought maybe you could track down the owner. It was pretty unusual Tom, has a gold-plated handle with jewels on it," I explained. "Anyway, it sure as hell didn't belong to me, and I didn't put my name on the return address if that's what you mean."

"It won't matter, they'll trace it back to you just the same."

"Maybe so, but that will take a while. In the meantime, I'm going to find Bridgette's killer and put a couple of slugs into his sorry gut. Can you take the heat off me for a couple of days? I can't do my job if the police are on my back."

"No can-do Nick," he shouted. "You can't go off on your own half-cocked. The lieutenant already has orders out to bring you in for questioning."

"I can't come in until I have more to go on Tom. I'm in the dark right now, and the cards seem to be stacking up against me. Whoever did this has done a pretty fair job setting me up for the patsy role."

"You got anything to go on Nick?" He asked in a lowered tone.

"I got a plate. Could you run it for me Tom?" There was a long pause over the line. The operator came on and asked for another nickel, which I deposited. Tom was back on the line a second later.

"Give it to me," he relented. I pulled out the small scrap of paper Liam had provided.

"Washington, D.C. plate, Foreign Government, number 314," I read.

"You sure about that Nick?" he questioned skeptically.

"A witness took it down for me, but I'm pretty sure," I answered.

"What witness?" he questioned.

"I've got to run Tom. I'll check in with you later," I promised as I hung up the receiver. I stepped back out onto the sidewalk, then climbed back inside the DeSoto.

It took another ten minutes for the kid to come back, but he finally came running up aside of the car. He still had his newspaper bag slung over his shoulder. I rolled the passenger side window down and he stuck his head inside.

"How'd you make out kid?" I asked through the window. He looked over his shoulder, then reached slowly into his canvas bag and pulled out the 1911, along with a small box of ammunition. He handed them both over to me. I took the gun and tucked it away under my belt. "Nice job kid! Have any trouble?" He shook his head.

"It was like you said Mr. Chambers. There was a plain clothes cop sitting in the downstairs lobby," he reported proudly. "I knew right away cause he was sitting in a chair with a paper over his face, just like they do in the movies. I could tell right away since it was yesterday's paper, ya see? Well anyway, he saw me heading for the stairway and flashed his badge at me, then asked what I was doing in the building."

"What did you say?"

"I told him I got my deliveries to make and then tried to sell him the morning edition. Well, he shooed me off real quick and I headed right upstairs. It was pretty simple after that. The gun was where you said it was, and nobody saw me go in or out of your office," he reported proudly.

"Nice job kid," I commented. "You got my number so keep your eyes open and call me if you see anything else." He nodded and tossed a paper on the front seat.

"Looks like you made the news," he reported as he walked off to sell more of his inventory.

I unfolded the paper and read the front page. It was a small by-line about halfway down.

Local Woman Found Dead

A young woman identified as Bridgette Hendricks was found dead in her workplace on the third floor of a downtown office building early yesterday morning. The police are classifying her death as suspicious. Her employer, one Nicholas Chambers, Private Investigator is wanted for questioning.

I put the car into gear and drove away slowly.

Seven: The Turks Head Club

The Turks Head building was just a few blocks away, but I really needed to get out of sight before some over-ambitious cop eyeballed my plate and pulled me over. I took a chance and parked the Desoto behind an old dumpster in an alleyway one block down from the Building. The Turks Head Building was a sixteen-story high-rise on the corner of Westminster and Weybosset St. The building had inherited its unique name from the old shop-keeper who had owned the land before its construction. He had mounted a ship's figurehead of a Sultan above his store to attract customers. When the new building was constructed, a replica of the old Turks head was mounted on the side of the building in stone. As I approached the entrance, I looked up at the ominous figure looming overhead. He seemed to be watching over the entire city, ready to defend her from hostile marauders. I passed cautiously beneath, through the main entranceway and into the spacious first floor lobby.

I knew that the Turks Head Club was on the top floor of the lofty building. An aging security guard stopped me at the lobby desk to ask what my business was. I told him I had an appointment with my attorney on the fifth floor and he let me pass. I entered the elevator and rode it up to the sixteenth floor.

When the heavy brass door rolled open, a stern-faced woman at the reception desk gave me the evil eye as soon as I stepped off. It was the kind of look designed to make you turn-a-round if you really didn't belong. She was in her early thirties with black hair waved back in an Italian cut with short curls. She wore a smart maroon tweed jacket with matching skirt. A short string of white pearls hung from her narrow neck, her shoulders were squared and padded. She was an attractive woman under the uniform, with jade eyes and a nice figure from what I could see behind the large mahogany desk. A set of black cat glasses rested on her nose and her eyes peered through them at me.

"Good morning Sir, how can we help you?" she asked as she eyed me up and down. I suddenly became conscious of my inadequate attire, then straightened my tie as I approached the principles desk.

"I'm interested in a membership," I replied. She looked me over again somewhat doubtfully, then lifted the receiver on her telephone. She pushed a buzzer and spoke into the mouthpiece.

"A Gentleman is here inquiring about a membership sir," she explained to the person on the other end. She nodded and looked back up at me.

"Did you have an appointment Sir?" she questioned as though she didn't already know the answer. I ignored the question.

"I was referred for membership by Mr. Preston Scott. He spoke very highly of this establishment and encouraged me to drop in the next time I had the yacht in Newport," I stated arrogantly. I was pretty sure Preston Scott was a member as he had asked me to call him at the Turks Head Club one evening to update him on the case.

"Oh… You live in Newport?" she asked with an elevated degree of interest.

"Only in the summer. We have a small villa out on Brenton Point, but most of the year we stay at the family estate in Edenborough," I answered.

"Edenborough Scotland?" she asked.

"Of course," I replied pretentiously.

"What is your name Sir?"

"Johnathon Swift, the third" I answered. She turned on her swivel chair and whispered the rest of the conversation into the mouthpiece with her back to me. A moment later the chair spun back around, and she hung up the receiver.

"Mr. Fitzgerald will see you Mr. Swift. He asked that you please have a seat in the reception lounge. He'll be with you shortly. That's the third door on the right," she instructed.

"Very good," I replied. I strolled down the hallway and went into the third room on the right. The room was exactly what you would expect to see in a private gentleman's club. The floor was a polished mahogany parquet, the walls paneled ceiling to floor in dark oak, half a dozen low coffee tables with high-backed leather smoking chairs, a few gilded framed paintings, which looked to be from the Renaissance period. I took a seat at one of the coffee tables, pulled out a smoke and set it on fire.

A few minutes later a tall elderly gentleman entered the room and greeted me with a warm handshake. He took the seat aside of me.

"Very nice to make your acquaintance Mr. Swift," he greeted. "I must say your dropping by like this is a bit unusual, but if Preston has referred you, we certainly want to get to know you better. You say you're interested in a membership?" he questioned.

"Certainly," I answered. "Why Preston couldn't say enough good things about this establishment. He said anyone who's anyone is a member here, and if I don't mind saying so, I'm someone."

"I assuming he's offered to sponsor you Mr. Scott?" he asked. "You realize that all of our members are sponsored during their first year of membership. Actually, the club requires two sponsors for each new member Mr. Swift."

"Of course Preston did offer to sponsor me, but I hadn't realized that two sponsors were needed Mr. Fitzgerald. Perhaps if you showed me your membership list, I could identify another member whom I'm acquainted with?" I suggested.

"That wouldn't be possible Mr. Swift as our membership list is strictly confidential," he explained. I took another drag on my smoke and waited without responding. It was a behavior I had noticed with most of my spoiled rich clients. When someone told them something they didn't want to hear, they simply didn't respond and waited for a different answer.

"Well, I suppose that leaves me out then," I replied finally, snuffing my smoke out in the ashtray. "It's a shame though. I was prepared to make a handsome donation to the club." He spoke up just as I began to stand.

"Sometimes we make special exceptions for special applicants Mr. Swift. I might be persuaded to sponsor you myself," he offered.

"Would you? That would be most gracious of you Mr. Fitzgerald."

"Perhaps you could complete an application," he suggested, lifting a small folio out from underneath the table. He handed the file over to me. "I assume the annual membership fee will not be a problem?" He asked.

"Certainly not," I replied. "If you'll just let me know the amount, I'll have my secretary courier a check over today," I offered.

"Five thousand dollars," he replied. I was taken back by the obscene amount and wanted to tell him just how ridiculous it was, but I kept my head.

"You'll have it by this afternoon," I promised.

"Very good! Please take your time and complete the application Mr. Swift. I'll give you some privacy now," he offered as he stood up from his chair. I stood up with him and shook his hand again.

"Thank you," I replied.

"When you've completed your application, just leave it with Estelle at the reception desk. The membership committee will review it within the week and make their decision. But I shouldn't imagine there will be any problem Mr. Swift. Please be sure to list me as your second sponsor," he reminded me as he walked from the room.

I sat back down and went to work on my fictional application. In some ways it was a typical club membership application with the usual questions for address, telephone number, and employer (if applicable). But this application had separate sections for winter and summer residences, tobacco and alcohol preference, and any other special requests the member may have of the club. For personal references I listed Governor Pastore, a U.S. Senator, and the Crown Prince of Balah (wherever that was). Under annual income I simply wrote "Trust fund." The last question on the application was personal net worth. I thought for a moment not wanting to over-play my hand, then jotted down $312 million. The only item on the application that wasn't fabricated was my telephone number. I wanted them to call me back.

I walked the application back out to the reception area and saw that Estelle had left her desk, so I placed the portfolio down on the desk blotter and started for the elevator. While I was waiting, I glanced at the door closest to the elevator. A gold leaf sign above it read *"Board of Directors."* The elevator door rolled open suddenly. I looked across at the reception area and saw that Estelle still had not returned to her desk. Before the elevator door had closed I had made my way into the Board room, shutting the door behind me.

The room was long and narrow with three lofty windows on the far wall that looked down over the city. The centerpiece was an immense polished mahogany table that spanned two thirds of the room. I counted twenty-four high-backed leather chairs gathered around it. There were at least two dozen portraits of distinguished men from various periods in time hanging on the oak walls. Each portrait had a gold label affixed to the bottom of its gilded frame. The label showed the man's name and the years in which he presumably served as President. The portraits seemed to go back further then the buildings construction.

On the wall closest to the hallway were photographs of each Board of Directors, arranged by year of service. I went to the most current photograph (1947) and scanned across the image of twenty-four men standing in front of a large flagstone fireplace. The first initial and last name of each man was inscribed on the lower section of the photo.

My heart skipped a beat as I noticed a man standing in the front row, fifth from the left. He was a short man with short black greased back hair. He had a thin handlebar moustache. He was holding a cane in his right hand. I counted over five names from the left; *I. Demidov*. I burned the face into my mind. Suddenly a woman's voice echoed out from behind me.

"Mr. Swift?" she stated. "This area is for members only," she scolded. I turned and smiled at her.

"My apologies," I replied. "I was waiting for the elevator to come up and got a glimpse through the door of this beautiful crown molding. I simply had to get a closer look at it. Terribly sorry, I certainly didn't mean to break any rules. Such impeccable workmanship," I complemented as I stepped back out into the hallway. She closed the door behind me. I walked back to the elevator and pushed the down button. Estelle sat back down at her desk.

"Mr. Fitzgerald mentioned the Board would need to approve my membership, do you happen to know when their next meeting would be?" I asked.

"The Board is meeting tomorrow night Mr. Swift, but it's actually our Membership Committee who needs to approve your application, and they won't be meeting for another two weeks. So, I wouldn't expect a response until close to month-end," she explained. The elevator door rolled open and I stepped inside.

"Thank you for your help Estelle. I hope that we see each other again sometime," I commented as the elevator door rolled shut. As the car descended sixteen floors a smile gradually took over my face. I had a last name now, and a face that was burned into my memory. *Isaac Demidov*, it was just a name, but that was all I needed. I would find Mr. Demidov and when I did it would be payback time, and I wouldn't be paying him in currency.

Eight: An Old Friend

When you're in trouble, real trouble, you lean on the people you trust most in life. The people who will help you regardless of detriment to themselves. I was in a real jam this time. Bridgette had been brutally murdered, and the police were looking in my direction. If I didn't come up with some answers fast, I'd be looking to solve her murder from behind bars. There were three people that I really trusted. One was a priest, the second was a buddy from the old neighborhood, and the third was a woman I hadn't seen in nearly three years.

My buddy from the old neighborhood owned a small coin and antique store over in Olneyville. I had an idea he might be able to help me with something, so I drove in that direction. Ten minutes later I was pulling up onto the curb outside of his shop. I stepped out from the car and looked up at the sign hanging over the front entrance.

Sully's Curiosity Shop
Guns, Jewelry, Diamonds, Tackle, Musical Instruments Bought, Sold, Exchanged

I opened the door and walked inside. A brass bell announced my entrance.

"Nick! You old dog!" a voice echoed out. The voice belonged to a tall middle-aged man standing behind the counter. A smouldering cigar hung loosely from his unshaven face.

"Hey Sully," I replied. As I approached him, I noticed his hand riding a sawed-off double barrel shotgun mounted under the countertop. He lifted his hand to shake mine but saw that I had noticed the gun.

"Can't be too careful these days Nick," he explained. "Neighborhood isn't what it used to be. I've been robbed twice this past month. Just some neighborhood punks who linger out in front of the store. When they see me go in back to use the restroom, they sneak inside and help themselves to some merchandise. Trying to make a sap out of me I tell ya. If I see any of those punks again, they'll get a complimentary round of buckshot in their backsides. But what brings you over to the west side Nick?"

"I'm wondering if you can help me with something Sul?" I asked.

"I'll do my best," he replied.

"Got a pad and pencil?" I asked. He nodded and walked off into the back of the store. I thought for a moment of steeling something and running off, but I really needed the information. A minute later he re-emerged with a small white pad and pencil in hand. He placed them both down on the countertop in front of me.

"What gives?" he asked.

"Give me a second pal," I replied. I took the pencil and paper and started sketching the knife I had found in my freezer the night before. I drew it as best as I could from memory. The straight razor-sharp steel blade that narrowed at the end, the polished jewelled golden handle, the unusual symbol engraved on the hilt. After a minute, I had sketched out a fair representation of the weapon. I pushed the pad across the counter back at him. He picked it up and examined the rudimentary drawing.

"Looks Russian Nick," he remarked. "A little like a Russian Kindal dagger, but this looks like a custom piece. It's a pretty unique blade, especially the handle, what was it made of?" he asked.

"Gold," I answered. Polished with four ruby's embedded in it. Does the symbol mean anything to you?" He stared hard at it for a minute or so.

"Nope… sorry pal," he replied.

"How about the name *Isaac Demidov*? Does that mean anything to you?" I questioned.

"Can't say that it does, but I can ask around if you like?" He offered. I nodded.

"Ok, thanks Sul. Keep the drawing and give me a call if you come up with anything," I instructed.

"Sure, but how about some fire power Nick? You need me to fix you up with anything? I got a couple nice M1 30 cal Carbines in the back. If that's not enough, I just took in a beautiful 1930 Vickers-Maxim Mark I machine gun, tripod and all. It might be a little hard to find ammo, but I can set you up with some if you're interested?" he asked.

"I'll pass for now Sully, but if I change my mind I know who to call."

He shook my hand and I walked back outside. The sky had gone gray and a wall of heavy dark clouds was approaching from the west. A storm was on its way.

Nine: St. Annes Cemetary

I got in my car and headed west out of town. I knew I was pressing my luck staying in Providence, and that it was only a matter of time before Tom sent his dogs out after me. I wasn't exactly sure where I was headed to, but knew I needed to get clear of the City. I left Olneyville and drove south down Cranston Street into Knightsville.

I was a couple of miles in before I noticed him. He was keeping a few cars behind in a black coupe and sticking with me on the turns. He was good, staying close enough not to lose sight of me, but not so close that I would notice him. But noticing people was my business, and I was already keeping one eye out for the police. I pulled over at a corner drug store and bought a fresh pack of smokes, then glanced out the window before heading back outside. He was parked about a block away in front of the Brewery. I walked back outside, got in the car and drove off.

I kept my eye in the rear-view mirror as I pulled away. He waited for a moment, then slid out of his parking spot just as I was making the turn onto

Cranston Street. I drove down Cranston Street and took a glance back as I approached St. Mary's Church. The coupe had disappeared.

I had an idea and drove straight into the parish cemetery. St. Mary's Cemetery was an expansive multi-acre cemetery stretching close to a mile along Dyer Pond. I drove half that distance through the property before pulling over and parking the Desoto. I stepped out and walked up to a headstone, went down on one knee and blessed myself. I looked over my left shoulder in the direction of the entrance gate. It took about a minute before the black coupe drove inside. I drew the 1911 from under my belt, pulled the slide back to chamber a round and waited. The car drove slowly along far side of the property, staying a safe distance from my sedan, then stopped about 50 yards off and shut its engine down.

I turned forward towards the headstone and bowed my head down a little. I heard a door open and shut on the coupe. Then footsteps on the road behind me. The footsteps were slow and deliberate, and heading in my direction. I eased my index finger in front of the trigger on the automatic. The footsteps were drawing closer to me now. Twenty feet, fifteen, ten, five feet... I spun quickly and drew the gun out in front of me.

"That's close enough!" I shouted. I thought for a moment that I was seeing a ghost. She was standing a few feet away from me, wearing a London Fog trench coat that hugged her full figure in a nice way and hung just above her knees. She had copper brown hair with soft chestnut eyes. She wasn't carrying a weapon. We stood there for an awkward moment not saying anything to one another

"Nick?" she finally questioned looking down at the 1911 that was still in my hand and pointing directly at her. I lowered the gun, eased the hammer back down with my thumb, and tucked it away under my belt. "Thank you," she added in grateful appreciation.

"You're welcome," I replied.

"I realize it's been some time Nick," she spoke in a warm British accent. Alexandra Watson was a British agent who had helped me out of a jam on a case overseas a few years back. We had gotten to know one another even better once the case had ended, but her work called her home and I hadn't seen her in nearly three years.

"Alex," I said, not knowing exactly what to say.

"I nearly lost you at that turn back there and had to double back," she explained.

"What are you doing here, and what's with the tail job anyway?" I questioned. She smiled back at me.

"I happened to be in the area on business and noticed your name in the paper this morning," she explained. "I'm sorry I was following you Nick. I suppose it's just a force of habit, waiting for the right time... I'm also terribly sorry to hear about Bridgette," she added. I nodded back. She walked up and hugged me. I was still a little numb, but after a moment I hugged her back. A minute passed as we held onto each other without speaking. When we finally let go, I looked into her soft chestnut eyes. They were still beautiful, but they seemed to have somehow grown tired and weary since the last time I had seen them.

"Maybe we can grab a cup of coffee somewhere and catch up Nick?" she suggested.

"Sure," I replied. "Follow me and we'll head over to Lindy's," I suggested. She nodded.

"Alright, but take it slow so I don't lose you this time," she joked. We got into our separate cars and drove out of the cemetery.

Ten: Lindy's Diner

Lindy's diner was a short drive from the cemetery. I led the way and Alex followed close behind. Seeing her again after all this time had thrown me a little. We had gotten pretty close before she left to go back to England, but I hadn't heard a word from her in the three years since. Her turning up now, only a day after Bridgette's death seemed strange to me. It was true that my name had been in the morning paper, but it seemed too coincidental that she would even be in the area after all this time. We pulled up to the diner and parked, then walked inside.

The place was nearly empty. Two tired looking electrical company workers sat in swivel stools at one end of the stainless-steel counter drinking coffee and eating hamburgers. An older woman sat alone in one of the window booths sipping a cup of afternoon tea and taking in the view. A taxi driver on his way out was paying his check with the cashier. Alex and I took a seat in one of the booths at the far end of the diner.

I pulled out my smokes and offered one to Alex. She took it and leaned across the table as I struck a match to it. Each of us waited for the other to say something. I finally broke the ice.

"Nice to know you're alive," I commented. I knew it was a low blow, but it needed to be said. Her soft brown eyes paned down at the table for a moment and then looked back up at me. There was a tear in one of them.

"I know how you must feel Nick. I felt the same way not being able to reach out to you all this time. I've been on an extended assignment overseas, and simply couldn't risk trying to get a post out," she explained.

"No mail in three years? It must be pretty rough over there," I said sardonically

"Yes, actually it was," she answered.

"Just where was this assignment?" I pressed. She drew some smoke into her lungs as if to buy time and think it over.

"In a country called Belarus. I've been there for the past three years Nick," she explained.

"Doing what exactly?" I asked. She smiled back at me.

"Working," she answered impatiently. "Working under-cover to be more precise Nick. I can't say much more about it than that." The waitress came up to our table. She was in her thirties, had powder blue eyes and a nice figure. Her hair was blonde and rolled back in victory curls. The tag on her shirt said her name was Patsy.

"Coffee?" she questioned. I nodded. Alex asked for some tea and she walked off. I started back in on Alex.

"So you've been working in Europe for the past three years, trapped in some under-developed country without a postal system, and now you just happen to be in Rhode Island a day after Bridgette is killed?" I questioned. She leaned back in her seat and crunched her forehead a little.

"You've become a lot more cynical since the last time we last saw each other Nick," she critiqued pulling some smoke in from her cigarette.

"Three years buys a lot of cynicism," I replied. "How about just playing it straight with me?"

"I'll be as honest as I can with you Nick," she answered. "I've been working on this particular assignment for the past three years. As a matter of fact, I'm still working on it. The details of which come under the subject of top secret. As it turns out, this job brought me to the states two weeks ago. We spent ten days down in Florida and took the train up to New England on Saturday."

"We?" I asked. She didn't reply to the question, implying that information came under the subject of top secret.

"You've been here for three days, and you didn't think to call?" I prodded. Her face painted red.

"I've been working Nick. I'm not here on holiday," she clarified. "I'm taking a chance just coming out here to meet with you. I read the article on Bridgette's death in the morning paper and thought there quite well may be a connection, and that I should do my best to warn you."

"Connection to what? Warn me about what?" I shot back. The waitress returned with our drinks and placed them down on the table along with a small tray with cream and sugar.

"Ready to order folks?" she asked, pulling a pencil out from one of her curls. "We have a nice meatloaf if you're hungry, and you can't go wrong with one of our burgers," she suggested.

"I'm fine with the tea?" Alex replied. Patsy turned in my direction looking somewhat disappointed.

"How about you fella?"

"I'll try the meatloaf with fries on the side," I ordered.

"Good choice?" she commented. She tucked the pencil away in her hair and walked off.

"Warn me about what?" I repeated.

"I can't get into any details with you Nick, other than to say you may be in danger," she explained. "I suggest you call your friend on the police force and ask for his protection," she advised.

"Protection from who?" I shot back. "The cops are already lining up to throw a net over me for Bridgette's murder. They'd lock me up as soon as I walked into the station."

"That might actually be the safest place for you right now Nick," she suggested. "The job I've been assigned to over the past few years is finally coming to fruition. There is something happening this week, here in the states. I'd like to know that you're safe in the meantime."

"What's happening?" I questioned. She tilted her head down at the table.

"I can't say Nick. It would compromise my operation, and your safety. You simply need to trust me," she explained.

"Trust you?" I shot back. "That's great coming from someone who disappeared for the past three years. All I know is someone killed Bridgette, and I plan on tracking him down. I've got a face and a name now, and before long I'll have payback. This guy made a big mistake, he just doesn't know it yet," I promised.

"You know who killed Bridgette?" she questioned.

"Do you?" I asked. Her eyes shot daggers across the table at me.

"Of course I don't Nick," she replied indignantly.

"Listen Alex, we can play this a couple ways. Either we come clean with one another and work together to take this scum bag down, or else there's not much more for us to talk about." She dropped her head and lifted it suddenly.

"You have no idea who you're dealing with Nick, and how dangerous these people are," she advised.

"I'm taking them down Alex, with or without your help. Whoever killed Bridgette is going to pay for what he did, and I plan on doing the collecting. The only thing this guy can count on is two lead slugs in his gut from me." She snubbed her cigarette out in the ashtray.

"I came here to warn you Nick, and I've done that. If you could only lie low for the next few days?" She questioned. I shook my head. She stood up from the table and put her hand on my shoulder.

"Take care of yourself Nick," she said before walking away. As she walked off the waitress approached with my lunch.

"Is your friend leaving?" she asked as she put the plate down in front of me.

"It looks that way," I replied stoically. "Could I get some ketchup?" She nodded and walked off. I noticed Alex glance back at me just before exiting through the front door. There was a look of distress in her eyes that hadn't been there the last time we had seen each other.

The meatloaf was as good as promised and I had cleaned the plate by the time the waitress brought my check over.

"You can pay at the register mister. Is there anything else I can get for you?" she asked. I glanced out the window and noticed two city cruisers pulling into the front lot. One of the squad cars pulled directly behind my Desoto, blocking me in.

"Got a bathroom I could use," I asked as the activity outside began to catch her attention. Two officers stepped out from their cars and began to look inside my DeSoto.

"Sure, end of the hall by the kitchen," she answered as she stared out the window at the activity going on out front. I lifted the check and got up from the booth, dropped it with a couple of bucks by the register, then headed for the restroom in back. There was a door to the bathroom on the right and a door at the end of the hall with an exit sign on it. I took the exit door and walked outside.

A worker for the Providence Journal was dropping a stack of evening bulletins in the lot behind the diner. I only had seconds before the two officers out front would make an appearance. The man rolled the back door down on his box truck, then walked up to the front cab. I ran to the back of the truck, lifted the door up a couple of feet and rolled myself inside, then pulled the door back down just as the truck shifted into gear and drove away. As we pulled away, I inched the door up and peered through the small opening back at the diner. We were just a block away when the two officers came rushing out from the rear exit with their guns drawn. I pulled the door down and sat up inside of the truck.

It was dark, so I pulled my pen light out and switched it on, then paned the beam around the interior. The truck was filled with tall stacked rows of heavy newspaper bundles. I climbed quietly up to the front and hid behind a stack closest to the cab.

I shut the light off and leaned back against the side of the box car, taking a moment to catch my breath. The Cranston Police were already on the lookout for me? How was that even possible? I suppose Tom could have lost patience and put out an APB, but Tom would have bought me a little time. Then it hit me… Alex. She could have tipped the authorities off while I sat there eating my lunch. She could have made an anonymous call to the police station and told them a murder suspect was eating lunch in Lindys Diner. She had suggested I turn myself in to stay safe. Maybe she decided to take matters into her own hands. It seemed I was a fugitive from justice now.

Eleven: Fugitive from Justice

Twenty minutes passed before the vehicle came to a stop. I felt the driver shift the transmission into park. I crouched down low and within a few seconds the rear door rolled open. Daylight invaded the interior of the truck. I heard the driver lift a few bundles out from the back, the door rolled down again, then a thump on the ground outside as he deposited his delivery. The cab door opened and closed, the gears shifted, and we were moving again.

This routine repeated itself a half dozen times over the next hour. I was getting nervous about the shrinking stacks of newspapers I had been hiding behind, and decided the next stop would have to be my last. The truck came to slow stop, and I waited for the driver to run through his routine one last time. This time when he opened the rear door, he stepped up inside of the truck bed. He spent a minute reorganizing a few stacks that were dangerously close to me, but by some stroke of luck he never noticed me. Eventually the door rolled shut and I heard his bundle hit the ground outside. I was up quickly and inched the rear door open to look outside. The coast seemed clear so lifted the door another foot or two and climbed out. I barely had time to close the door when the truck suddenly pulled away.

I looked around and saw that I was standing in the middle of an intersection, somewhere in a rural part of the state. My eyes were still adjusting to the sunlight as I stepped up onto the sidewalk. The sun was just beginning to set on the western horizon. There was a large cornfield across the street, which stretched for several blocks. I glanced up at the street sign on the corner that read *Scituate Ave.* There was a phone booth on the opposite side of the road under a dim street light that had just turned on. I walked across and stepped inside.

I had a name and a face that belonged to Bridgette's killer, but no easy way of tracking him down. My normal connections at the department would be useless now, and most of my informants were back in the city where I had to stay clear of. This led me back to every detective's first tool of the trade, the Bell Telephone book. I pulled the tattered copy out from the shelf beneath the phone. The cover had been torn off long ago, but the book itself was mostly intact.

I found my way to the D's and started thumbing through the pages. Da... De... Dem... About six pages in I finally reached the name *Demidov*.

There were three listings;

Peter Demidov, 25 Parkside Dr., Warwick.   IM-2260
Nicholas Demidov, MD., 1875 Park Ave, Cranston WI-2289
Dr. I. Demidov, 412 North Rd, Hope   *Unpublished*

The third name down caught my eye, *I. Demidov*. It could easily be Isaac Demidov, the same *I. Demidov* hanging on the wall in the Turks Head Club, the same scumbag who killed Bridgette, the same dirtball I planned to wreak havoc on. He was a doctor with an unpublished number, which indicated he might be wealthy enough to belong to the Turks Head Club. The address was only a few miles away. With any luck, I could make it by nightfall. I started walking west down Scituate Ave.

The sun was setting as I approached a small cape located at 412 North Rd in the quaint village of Hope. There was a sign post on the front lawn that read *Otto Demidov, DMD*. I wondered for a moment if the phone book had misprinted the listing, and if I had just walked several miles for no good reason. I went up on the front steps and noticed a *Closed* sign hanging in the jalousied storm door. I rang the bell, but no one answered, then looked down at my watch and saw it was a little after six-thirty. I needed to speak with this Otto Demidov to find out if Isaac Demidov ever lived or worked in the area. The hours on the window said the office would reopen at eight o'clock the next morning. If I planned to question Dr. Demidov, I would need a place to sleep for the night.

Twelve: The Red Lion Inn

I stepped down from the front door and walked back out to the sidewalk, then took a look around the small village. There was a spired church a block down the road, perched on an embankment of the Pawtuxet River. I started down the street and walked past as a handful of patrons were filing up a steep stairway on their way into evening mass. I turned and noticed a small sign across the road hanging above the front door to an old colonial. The sign read *The Red Lion Inn,* with a red lion standing watch above all who entered. I crossed over and went inside.

It was a small neighborhood tavern, the kind of out-of-the-way place where everyone turned around when a stranger like myself walks in. It was dimly lit with low hanging clouds of cigarette smoke lingering in the ceiling. There was a large wrap-a-round bar with an old timer standing patiently behind a well-worn oak countertop. A few small square tables with chairs were placed haphazardly up against the outer windows. The curtains on the windows were covered with a layer of dust. There was a phone booth up against the far wall. Two locals sat at the opposite end of the bar, smoking cigars and playing a hand of cards with one another. They gave me a passing glance as I sat down, then went back to their game. The bartender walked up and dropped a used coaster down in front of me.

"What will it be mister?" he asked.

"Scotch on the rocks," I ordered. I pulled a dollar from my wallet and placed it down on the countertop. "Could I get some change? I need to make a phone call," I explained. He took the dollar and returned a minute later with some loose change. I lifted two dimes from the countertop and walked over the telephone booth, stepped inside and closed the glass door. I needed to reach Tom to find out where I stood with the police. He would have left his office by now, but I might catch him at home. I dropped a dime in the coin slot and dialed his home number. The line rang twice before a soft female voice lifted the receiver on the other end.

"Hello?" she answered.

"Betsy… It's Nick Chambers," I greeted. "Is Tom home yet? It's important that I speak with him."

"He just came in the door Nick, one moment," she replied. I heard the receiver set down on a table, then some footsteps and voices whispering in the background. Within a minute Tom's heavy voice echoed over the line.

"Where in the hell are you Nick?" he shouted through the receiver. I ignored his question.

"What's going on Tom? Why were the Cranston Police trying to throw a net over me." I asked.

"I'll tell you what's going on pal! There's a warrant out for your arrest. A state-wide A.P.B. has been put out on you. You need to get your ass over here now, and I'll drive you down to the station myself," he instructed.

"You don't honestly think I killed Bridgette do you Tom?" I asked. There was a short pause over the line.

"No... Of course I don't Nick. But what I think doesn't mean shit. A judge issued a warrant for your arrest earlier today. The only information the rest of state law enforcement has is that a girl's been killed, had her throat cut, and one Nick Chambers has been named as a suspect with a warrant out for his arrest. They've got you listed as armed and dangerous. Tell me you're not packing heat Nick?" he asked. I ignored the question again.

"That seems like pretty quick work to get a warrant written up already Tom?" I questioned.

"Well, your running from the police today didn't help your case much pal. Oh… and I got your little present in the mail this afternoon. I had to turn it over to evidence. The boys already tracked that little item back to the post office in Pawtuxet village, the one just below your apartment. That didn't help you very much either," he explained.

"Like I said earlier Tom, someone left that in my ice box for the police to find. I found it last night when I came home and figured it was better to get it out of my place," I explained.

"Maybe so, but it didn't look good for you just the same," he replied. "Now the boys think you're some sort of deranged maniac that likes to mail in his killing tools."

"Can't you see what's happening Tom? Two unknown witnesses from my building identify me leaving the place yesterday morning, the murder weapon ends up in my frozen foods, you receive instructions to search my place, and a warrant for my arrest is signed by a judge in record time… Somebody's setting me up, somebody very connected, and they're doing one hell of a good job at it."

"So you say Nick. Well come in and tell all of that to the Lieutenant, and I'll do what I can for you," he offered.

"I can't come in now the way things are stacked up against me Tom. I wouldn't stand a chance and you know it. My best bet is to do my job and find Bridgette's killer on my own."

"… and bring him in," he added for me. I let that remark drift in the air. "You got any leads yet?" he questioned. I thought about it for a moment and knew I had to give him something to keep his confidence.

"A witness saw a man leaving my building and getting into a car a little after nine yesterday morning," I reported. "He gave me a pretty decent description of the car and I was able to track down a name to go with it."

"Is that the plate you had me run down? Who was witness anyway?" he asked.

"Yeah, same car, but the witness doesn't matter," I answered.

"All right then… Just give me the name of the owner and I'll check him out for you," he offered.

"I can't have the police spooking this guy on me Tom," I answered. "I'm working a lead right now, and I should have something I can hand over to you within twenty-four hours." I heard a growl over the line.

"How in the hell am I supposed to help you Nick if you keep giving me nothing to go on!" He barked impatiently.

"Did you have any luck with that plate?" I asked. He paused for a moment.

"Yeah, as a matter of fact I did. I know it's probably hard for you to imagine Nick, but the police are actually capable of finding out information on rare occasions," he answered cynically.

"What did you find out?" I pressed.

"It's a diplomatic plate."

"I figured that much out for myself Tom," I interrupted. "Is that all?"

"Give me a second," he shouted back. "I wasn't able to get a name on the owner, not without a warrant at least, and I didn't have a warrant smart ass. I did find out that the plate is one of several belonging to a foreign embassy in Washington, D.C."

"Foreign embassy? Let me take a guess... Belarus?" I questioned. The line went quiet for a moment.

"Now how in the hell did you know that Nick?" he bellowed over the line.

"Like I said, I've been busy working Tom," I answered. "Did you find anything else?"

"An address to the embassy," he replied. "619 New Hampshire Avenue, District of Columbia. Are you telling me that a car from the Belarus Embassy in Washington D.C. was seen leaving your building early yesterday morning?" I hung the receiver up.

I stepped out from the phone booth and walked back up to bar. My scotch was waiting patiently for me. I sat down and took a slug from the highball. I was taking a chance not filling Tom in completely on everything that I had discovered, but I was on the trail now and couldn't afford to have the cops mucking things up on me. If there was a state-wide APB out on me, that would make things more difficult, but I needed to push forward just the same. I nodded my head at the bartender, and he came back over.

"Yeah mister?" he asked.

"Wonder if I could get a little grub?"   He nodded and pulled a small pad from underneath his apron.

"Sure. We got hamburgers and corned beef sandwiches on the menu tonight," he reported.

"I'll take a corned beef sandwich," I replied. He nodded and jotted my order down on his pad.   "I drove all the way down from Boston to see my dentist, but he was closed by the time I got here. I was wondering if you had a room available?" He smiled and nodded back at me.

"Sure, we got a few vacancies upstairs?" He smiled.

"How much?" I asked.

"Since you're already having dinner here, let's say two bucks?" I nodded and took another drink from the highball. He smiled and walked off with my order. He left the bar and walked into a back room that I assumed was a small kitchen. I checked my wallet and saw that I had a little over eight dollars, along with some pocket change.

Ten minutes later the old man re-emerged from the kitchen holding a small plate in his hand, which he carried back behind the bar.

"Here you go mister," he said as he placed the sandwich down in front of me. "So you got a bad tooth do ya?" he asked.

"Yeah," I replied rubbing my jaw. "It's been aching for weeks, and I've put it off," I explained. He laughed and nodded back.

"Well Doc Demidov should fix you up," he replied. "Been to see him a few times myself, and he done a really good job on me. Course, I just got myself a full set of dentures last year, so I don't expect to see him much anymore."

"Do you know if there was a medical doctor in that office at one time?" I asked. He answered the question right away.

"Oh yeah... That was a few years back. I think he was a cousin or brother of the dentist. Had the same last name, and I seem to remember the first name was Ivan or something along that line," he explained. "Course I never saw him myself as a patient, I've seen old Doc Jablow for most of my life. But you're right mister, there was a medical doctor there before the dentist moved in."

"You say that was about three years ago?" He nodded back. "What happened to the doctor?" I asked.

"That was the funny part," he noted. "Just up'd and left one day without telling any of his patients. Nobody really knows where he went. A few months after he disappeared, the dentist moved in. Since he has the same last name, we all figured it's a brother or cousin maybe. Why, do you need a doctor too? I'd be happy to refer you to Dr. Jablow?"

"It's nothing urgent. I just thought while I was here, maybe I'd kill two birds with one stone." He nodded.

"It's tough to get old, ain't it mister?" I nodded back and laughed. He walked off and left me to my sandwich. I inhaled the corned beef and drank a second highball for Bridgette. It was a little after nine o'clock when the bartender dropped my check down on the countertop.

"You want to pay for the room now mister?" he asked in a way that implied it was preferable. I nodded that I would.

"Sure, why not," I answered.

"That will bring your bill to three dollars and fifty cents," he remarked. I pulled four dollars from my wallet and placed it down on the countertop. He lifted the cash from the counter and replaced it with a small room key.

"Room's up the stairs there on the left. There's a bathroom too if you need to clean up. I'll just need your name for the register?" he asked.

"Walter Johnson," I answered. He nodded and jotted my fictitious name down on his little pad. I drank down what was left of the scotch and headed up the rear stairway, then used the key he had given me to unlock the room on the second floor.

It was a pathetic little musty room with a twin bed and small window that peered out over Main Street. The kind of room that a drunk would be happy to sleep in after a long night downstairs, but one that a sober man wouldn't be caught dead in. I was somewhere in between, but happy to have a roof over my head tonight. I locked the door behind me, walked over and cracked the window, then sat down on the old bed. I could feel the springs pushing up through the tired mattress, but I was in no position to complain to the old innkeeper. A cool breeze drifted into the stale room. I could smell rain in the air now, and within a few minutes it broke loose outside. I reached over and pulled the window down a few inches, leaving it open just enough to maintain the flow of fresh oxygen. I leaned back on the bed, resting my head in a soft down pillow. My eyelids rolled shut and the room went dark.

Thirteen: A Visit with the Dentist

The rain was still falling steady when I woke the next morning. I had slept surprisingly well in the old bed and was feeling better. I used the half bathroom in the hallway to clean up as much as I could, then put my jacket on and went downstairs. The tavern on the first floor was dark and empty now. I passed through it and headed outside onto a small front porch, which overlooked Main Street. I stopped to have a smoke and take in the early morning downpour. I looked at my watch and saw that it was a few minutes after nine, but much of the small town still seemed to be sleeping. An occasional car drove past in the rain as I stood there breathing in the soggy morning air. I looked down the road at the small dental office. There was a light on inside now. I checked the time again and saw it was just nine-thirty. I tossed what was left of my cigarette over the porch rail and started across the street.

A brass bell rang above my head as I entered the front door of the small office. There was no one at the receptionist desk, so I sat down in the anti-room and waited. Within a few minutes I heard footsteps coming down the back stairway. An older man in a white lab coat stepped out into the waiting room.

"Good Morning Sir," he greeted in a Slavic accent I couldn't quite place. It could have been Russian or Ukrainian. He looked to be in his early sixties, with a tall lanky frame and short gray hair. "I am Dr. Demidov, how can I help you?" I stood up and shook his hand.

"I've had a bum tooth for some time Doc," I explained. "Just got to the point where I couldn't take it anymore, so I figured I'd better come in and have it looked at." He smiled and nodded back at me.

"Step into my examination room where I can get a better look at it," he instructed as he opened a door to the left of the empty reception desk. I walked inside. There was a dental chair at the room's center with lots of equipment surrounding it. A mirrored sideboard stood up against a wall with instruments laid out neatly on top. A radiator hissed against the opposite wall as if to warm me against the upcoming examination. "Please have a seat in the chair Mr.??" he questioned.

"Johnson, Walter Johnson," I replied. I took a seat in the examination chair and reclined back. Dr.

Demidov went over to the sideboard and retrieved a few stainless-steel instruments. He placed them down on the tray next to me.

"Any medical issues I should know about Mr. Johnson?" he questioned.

"No, nothing really doc. Although I was hoping to see my old physician while I was back in town. He used to practice in this office. He was a Dr. Demidov too. I'm guessing he's probably a relation of yours?" I questioned. A dubious look passed across his cold face.

"I believe you must mean Dr. Ivan Demidov," He replied. "I'm sorry to tell you that my cousin Ivan passed away three years ago Mr. Johnson. It was very unexpected," he explained. My heart sank for a moment. The name in the phone listing had been Ivan, not Isaac. Had I been on a wild goose chase?

"I'm sorry, I didn't know," I said not knowing what to say.

"I took over this office for my practice a few months after his death. Now where is that bad tooth of yours," he asked as he repositioned an overhead lamp to shine into my mouth.

"It's on the bottom right, second from the back Doc," I replied. The tooth had been bothering me for some time, but the pain came and went so I left it alone. He stuck a small dental mirror into my mouth and repositioned the light to get a better view. He lifted a stainless-steel instrument from the tray that resembled a small ice pick with bent tip, then began using it to examine the bum tooth and I felt it. After a minute of probing and poking, he withdrew the primitive instrument from my month.

"I'm sorry to tell you this Mr. Johnston, but you have a bad cavity in your second molar. It should be easy enough to fill. Would you'd like to do that today?" He questioned.

"Sure Doc," I answered. He nodded. "I'm sorry to hear about Dr. Demidov," I commented. "He seemed like a competent physician. I still remember that cane he always walked around with, the one with the golden handle." He paused and shot a sudden suspicious look at me.

"I think you must be mistaken Mr. Johnson. My cousin Ivan never carried a cane. Are you sure you have the right physician?" he questioned.

"It could be my memory Doc," I replied. "I don't remember things the way I used too. I probably just have my physicians mixed up. Its been a while since I was here as a patient." He stood up and washed his hands.

"Just relax in the chair for a moment Mr. Johnson," he instructed. "I need to go to the medicine cabinet in the other room and prepare a Novocain injection for you, then we can begin the procedure." He walked from the room, closing the door on his way out.

I stood up from the chair and walked over to the door, put my ear up to the wood and listened. I could hear a phone dialing and then his voice speaking over the line.

"*It's Otto, I need to speak with him.*" A long pause followed. I cracked the door a half inch and peered through. The dentist was standing in front of a large oak side board, holding a phone up to his ear. His back was to me. Another minute passed before he spoke again. "*It's me… I have a new patient here asking questions about you,*" he explained to a third party on the other line. "*He say's his name is Johnson, but I've never seen him before.*" There was another long pause and then Otto spoke again. "*Of course, I'll take care of it cousin,*" he said before putting the receiver down.

He reached up and opened one of two large medicine cabinets hanging over the sideboard. He pulled down a bottle and took out a small glass syringe from one of the drawers. He screwed a needle onto the syringe, then turned the bottle upside down and drew some fluid into it. He put the bottle down and lifted the syringe up to the ceiling light, tapping it twice with his finger. I caught a quick glimpse of the label on the bottle. It was too far away to read the words, but I could make out one large symbol on the label, a skull and cross bones. He started to turn just as I closed the door and got back into the dental chair.

"Sorry for the delay Mr. Johnson," he greeted as he reentered the room. I had trouble finding the right size syringe for the injection." He walked up beside me and held the small needle in his right hand. "I'll administer a Novocain injection, then we'll give the medication ten or fifteen minutes to numb that molar," he explained. I noticed a bead of sweat rolling down his narrow forehead as he leaned over me. There was a slight tremor in the hand holding the syringe.

As he started to reach for my mouth, I grabbed at the wrist holding the syringe and stood up, pushing him back against the wall. We struggled with one another for nearly a minute, knocking over the tray of stainless instruments. He was stronger than I expected, but I began to win the battle and the small needle started to inch closer to his neck. His glasses were cock-eyed on his face now, and he was struggling to see clearly, but still fighting back.

Finally, the needle eased into his neck, passing inside his jugular. I pushed the plunger on the syringe, and he let go of his grip on me. I stepped backwards away from him.

"What's the matter Doc?" I asked. "It's just a little Novocain, right?" He fell to the ground and sat upright against the wall. His face went pale and his eyes rolled back inside his head. His body began to convulse as his back arched dramatically. After a minute he went limp and dropped to the ground. I knelt down beside him and felt on his throat for a pulse. There wasn't one.

I walked back out into the waiting area and took a look at the bottle he had left behind on the sideboard. The label on it read *Strychnine*. I lifted the telephone and rang the operator. A pleasant female voice came over the line.

"Operator, how may I help you?" she greeted politely. I spoke into the receiver.

"Operator, I was just on a call but was somehow disconnected. Would you mind placing the call again for me," I asked.

"Of course Sir, that was the Washington exchange," she confirmed. The line clicked and a few seconds later began to ring. The line rang three times on the other end before a soft female voice answered it.

"Good morning… Embassy of the Republic of Belarus," a woman's voice greeted in broken English. I hung up the receiver.

I looked down at the sideboard and noticed a small address book. It was lying half-opened on the top shelf. I picked it up and saw it had been left open to the letter I. There were only three entries on the page. Two were women's names; Ingrid Baxter, and Irene Comstock. The third was a man's name,

Isaac Demidov, Belarus Embassy, Washington, D.C.

I tore the page from the address book and tucked it away in my pocket, then noticed a small tin box in one of the top shelves with the words *petty cash* markered on the lid. I opened the box and counted a total of fifty-three dollars inside, mostly ones and fives. I did what any self-respecting fugitive would do and pocketed the cash.

Fourteen: Union Station

I exited the office through the front door and flipped the window sign over to show *Closed*, then looked up and down the street, but the village still looked empty. Rain was still pouring down hard outside as I stood under the small portico. I lit a smoke, then tipped my hat down over my forehead to hide my face. I had just killed a man and stolen money from his office. Sure, it was in self-defense but I was the only one who knew that.

It was only a matter of time before I would be identified. Once the body was discovered, the news would spread quickly throughout the small village. The innkeeper would remember a stranger by the name of Johnston who had stayed at his tavern the night before and who had been asking questions about the dentist. The police would get a description of the stranger from the innkeeper and would put two and two together. There was already an APB out on me, and a second killing would only solidify the DA's case against me. The dentist had tried to put me to sleep for good, but there was no way for me to prove that to anyone. I needed to get to the bottom of what was going on, and I was on borrowed time now.

I glanced around the corner of the building and noticed a small garage out back. I ran down the steps and along the drive into the back yard, then pulled open a set of split garage doors to look inside. There was a pickup parked inside, which I assumed belonged to the dentist. I stepped in and closed the doors behind me.

The rain was knocking hard on the roof above. I pulled out my flashlight and waved the beam at the old truck. It was a thirty-five or thirty-six Ford. There was a tool bench at the back of the garage where I found a small screwdriver. I got into the truck and used the driver to pry open the ignition switch, then touched the two wires together and the engine turned over. There was an old leather jacket on the front seat. I took off my coat and tossed it in back, then put on the jerkin. I stepped back out and opened the garage doors, got back inside and drove out.

I wasn't exactly sure where I was headed to. I only knew I needed to put some distance between myself and the small town of Hope. Dr. Otto Demidov had clearly lied to me. The man I was looking for was his cousin. The number he had called was a Washington exchange, which tied to the info that Tom had given on the license plate of the Packard Liam had spotted. I was on the right track now and I had the name of Bridgette's killer, *Isaac Demidov*. He was at the Belarus Embassy in Washington, D.C., so that's where I would go.

I glanced down at the gas gauge on the old Ford. There was half a tank remaining. I'd try for a train station and buy a ticket to D.C. Any station in Rhode Island was out of the question now. The state police had most likely been alerted and would be on the lookout for me. I'd have to drive to Connecticut and catch a train from there. I took a right onto Route 117 and drove west. The rain was pouring down and I was inside an old pickup, which was probably the best cover I could hope for.

I drove for an hour before stopping at a gas station to fill the tank. I asked the attendant for a pack of smokes and a newspaper. He ran back inside and a minute later came back out carrying both.

"That's six dollars, including the gas mister," he said as he passed the cigarettes through my window. I handed him six dollars and an extra quarter for his trouble, said thanks and drove off. I opened the paper and scanned the front page. To my relief my photo wasn't on it. I tossed it down on the seat and drove on.

Another hour passed before I reached the Thames River Bridge in New London, Connecticut. As I went across, I glanced down the river into a heavy fog that was rolling in from the Atlantic Ocean. Once over the bridge, I drove down the west bank of the river in the direction of Union Station, then parked the Ford in an empty lot across the street. I sat in the truck for some time, watching people pass in and out of the station, just to be sure it was clear of law enforcement. When enough time had passed, I stepped out from the truck and crossed the street, then went into the old station.

The New London station didn't have the kind of lavish interior you found in the grand train stations of New York or San Francisco. It was more of a practical station, the type you see in small town America. The ticket booths were located on the outside wall just as you walked into the building. Flaking paint on interior walls reached up to a lofty overhead ceiling supported by oak rafters. A lunch counter with empty swivel stools was built along the rear wall of the station. A set of lonely lockers stood at attention near the entrance to the rest rooms. I walked up to one of the ticket booths and pulled out my wallet.

"What time is the next train to D.C.?" I questioned to a middle-aged man behind the wire window. He instinctually glanced over his shoulder at a small Westinghouse clock hanging on the wall behind him, then turned back to me.

"It's a quarter past three now mister," he reported. "I'm afraid you just missed it. The next train doesn't leave until seven o'clock this evening. It's an overnight train and should arrive in Washington D.C first thing in the morning," he explained.

"It's for me," I replied. "How much?" He ran his pencil down his rate sheet.

"Sleeper car is all sold out, so you'll have to ride in coach. A dollar and ten cents please," he prompted. I slid two dollars under the window, and he passed back a ticket along with my change. "Name please?" he asked while pressing a pencil to his passenger log.

"Michael Jamison," I answered, deciding it was time for another name change.

"Looks like you've got a few hours to burn Mr. Jamison. The lunch counter is across the way if you're hungry, and the restrooms are over there on the left," he suggested.

"Is there a department store nearby?" I asked. He nodded and pointed over his shoulder.

"Just go across the road and head up State Street. Genung's Department Store is a couple of blocks on the right. I nodded and walked off.

I used the restroom and wrapped the forty-five up in an old cleaning rag I had found on the window sill. I walked back out and dropped a nickel in one of the lockers, then discreetly slipped the wrapped gun along with the truck keys inside. I put the locker key in my pocket and headed back outside.

I crossed over and headed up the road as the attendant had directed. Genung's Department Store was exactly where he had said it would be. There was a small barber shop on the opposite side of the road and I needed a shave in a bad way. I crossed over and went inside the small shop.

The barber was leaning back in one of the chairs reading a newspaper, waiting for his next client. He jumped to attention when I walked inside. He was in his forties, average height with short dark hair and a thin Ronald Coleman moustache. He had the look and build of an ex-military man.

"Afternoon!" He greeted with a smile. "Need a cut?" He asked. I nodded and hung my new leather jacket up on the wall hook.

"And a shave if you have time?" I replied.

"Nothing but time mister," he commented with a smile. "Have a seat," he instructed as he wiped the swivel chair down with a white towel he had slung over his shoulder. I took a seat and he draped a sheet over my shoulders, then went to work with his comb and scissors. "From around here?" he asked.

"No... I had a bit of layover down at the station and thought I'd take a walk around town," I explained without saying where I was from.

"That so, traveling by train? Where ya headed to?" he asked.

"Washington, D.C." I answered.

"That so... Just took the wife down there last year," he reported. "We saw almost all the sites. The Jefferson Memorial, the White House, the Smithsonian... Oh yeah, and the Washington Monument. That staircase up to the top was something else, but you can see the whole city once you get up there. Great place to visit if you get the chance. You plan to do much site seeing while you're down there?" He asked.

"No, I'm just going down on business," I replied.

"Yeah, what line of business you in?" he asked. I thought to myself this guy would make a great detective.

"I'm in sales," I answered. "Soaps and detergents. We sell to all the big department stores," I explained. He nodded without seeming that interested.

When he had finished cutting my hair, he pulled the sheet from my shoulders, shook the cut hair off and tucked it back under my collar in front, then spackled some warm shaving cream on my face and neck. He pulled a straight razor from the drawer and ran it up and down a long leather strap half a dozen times, then started to work. He was skilled with the blade and shaved my face in under a minute, then finished up on the back of my neck. When he was done, he powdered some talcum on my neck and face and removed the sheet.

"All set mister," he said. "It's fifty cents for the cut and another quarter for the shave." I stood up, pulled my wallet out and handed him a buck. He took the bill and stepped over to the register to make change.

"Keep it," I said as I put the leather jacket on and walked back out into the rain. I jogged across the street and went into Genung's Department Store.

It was only October, but the winter merchandise was already on display and stocked high on the shelves. I headed upstairs to the Men's clothing section and found a pair of denim jeans and a plaid wool shirt. I needed to blend in now and not stand out in public. I picked up a small overnight bag, a tooth brush and some other essentials. There was a rack with some dime novels, so I picked up one by Micky Spillane called *I, the Jury*. It might help me to pass the time on the trip down. I rang everything out at the front register and headed back to the station.

Fifteen:
Train Ride
South

When I got back to the station I went into the restroom and changed into my new outfit. I threw my old clothes in the waste basket and headed back out to the lobby.

I took a seat at the lunch counter and waited for someone to come out from the back. After a few minutes an older woman in her sixties stepped out from the kitchen. She was short, plump, and wore a striped apron around her expansive waistline. Her white hair was pulled back in a net, her eyes slate gray. She placed a napkin and some silverware down on the countertop in front of me.

"Will you be having lunch or dinner Sir?" she asked. I looked up at the menu posted high on the wall.

"I'll take a turkey sandwich with fries," I ordered. "Is it possible to get a little scotch?" I asked. She let off a jolly laugh.

"No, I'm afraid not. It's strictly soda and water here, but you should be able to get a drink on the train once you board," she explained.

"I'll settle for a coke then," I answered. She wrote my order down on a small pad and walked back into the kitchen.

I spun my stool around and took a good look at the station. There were a handful passengers sitting on benches now in the center of the lobby. The same attendant that had sold me my ticket stood patiently on duty inside of his cage. I noticed several people waiting on the opposite side of the station under a sign that read *Arrivals*. After a few minutes, the old woman came out to deliver my sandwich, then poured me a soda from the fountain and brought it over.

"Anything else mister?" she asked.

"That should do it," I replied. She tore my check off her pad and placed it down on the countertop, then disappeared into the kitchen. She seemed to have some aversion to the front counter, I thought to myself. I looked up at the large clock hanging on the station wall. It was four-thirty.

At four forty-five a train pulled into the station and passengers began filing through the arrival doors. Most were greeted by family members who had been patiently waiting. They filed through the station and out onto the street to catch a cab or bus home. A few took seats in the lobby, waiting for the next train to arrive.

One passenger who sat down caught my eye almost immediately. She looked around thirty, a little over five feet in height, with short brown hair waved back on either side. She wore a white cotton shirt under a neat navy-blue button up jacket with padded shoulders. A matching pleated skirt hugged her hips and reached down just over her knees. She had a strikingly pretty face with soft brown eyes and blood red lipstick. I left some money on the counter, walked over to an empty bench along the rear wall and sat down.

I still had a couple of hours to burn before my train arrived, so I pulled out the dime novel and started into it. The sun was beginning to set outside as I read through the first few chapters. At some point the book fell onto my lap and I nodded off. I awoke later to a hand on my shoulder trying to rouse me.

"Hey Mr. Jamison," a voice in the darkness spoke. "That's your train outside, the one going to Washington." I opened my eyes and saw the ticket attendant standing in front of me. "You'd better get out there, they've already started to board," he reported. I stood up in my slumber, then grabbed my overnight bag and book off the bench.

"Thanks," I muttered, before heading quickly outside onto the train platform. There was a row of about twenty passengers that had formed aside of the train. I got in line and pulled my boarding pass from my pocket. The line was moving steadily as the conductor punched each passenger's ticket and helped them to board.

Suddenly two police officers stepped down from the train and stood beside the conductor. They seemed to be eyeing each passenger who boarded. The line moved forward another step as I tried to decide on what to do. Leaving the line now would only call attention to me. Another few steps forward… I was just six or seven people away now. I felt a bead of sweat roll down the side of my temple. Just then a woman's voice rang out from behind me.

"Don't leave without me Dear!" she shouted. I turned my head and saw the same attractive woman I had noticed in the station running up to me carrying a large suitcase. She came up and stood beside me in line, then went up on her heels to give me an extended kiss. As she did, I felt her slip something onto my left hand. I looked down and saw a gold wedding ring on my finger. We were next to board now and she held my hand tightly.

"You can't go on a honeymoon by yourself dear," she said as we approached the conductor. He took our tickets and was about to let us pass when one of the two officers who had been eye-balling me stepped up. I noticed his hand was resting on his gun holster.

"Good evening folks," he greeted. "Could I ask where you're headed to?" The woman wrapped her arm around my waist.

"Just got married yesterday officer," she said with a big smile and holding both of our hands for him to see the new set of golden rings. "We're on our way to Washington D.C. for our honeymoon," she explained as she fumbled with a plethora of site seeing brochures. She dropped a few at the officer's feet and he picked them up for her.

"Could I have your names please," the officer asked sceptically.

"I'm Michael Jamison," I offered. She elbowed me in the ribs, hard enough for the officer to take notice.

"That's Mr. and Mrs. Michael Jamison if you please, and you better get used to saying it mister," she advised. "…and while we're at it, we may have only been married yesterday, but that's no excuse to make your wife carry the luggage," she scolded before dropping the heavy suitcase down on my foot. The officer laughed and waved us by. We stepped up onto the train and headed inside.

"Why don't you try and get us a table in the dining car dear. I'll bring our luggage to our compartment," she suggested. "I'm simply famished."

"Of course dear, whatever you say," I replied, handing the heavy suitcase and my overnight bag to her. I wasn't exactly sure what had just happened or for what reason, but her little act had got me by the police, and I was grateful for that. A sign pointed the way to the dining car at the rear of the train. My attractive new friend headed forward with her luggage.

I walked back through three cars before reaching the dining car. There was a steward standing immediately inside of the door. He was a tall narrow man without much meat on his bones. He had a heavy moustache and dark hair that was greased back on both sides. He held a stack of menus and silverware in his bony hands.

"One for Dinner?" he questioned.

"Two actually," I replied glancing unconsciously over my shoulder. "My wife should be right along."

"Very good Sir, please follow me," he instructed. He led me to the rear of the car and sat me at the last table on the right facing forward. Two other tables in the dining car were occupied. There was an older couple seated at a table up front, and a middle-aged overweight man seated alone in the middle of the car. The steward placed the menus and utensils down on the table. "Can I get you a drink while you wait Sir?" he asked.

"You can," I replied. "I'll take a scotch, no ice."

"And your wife?" he asked.

"Gin and tonic," I order. He nodded and walked off. I felt the train heave forward and looked out the window to my left. I could see lights from homes on the opposite side of the Thames River, and a few ship beacons dotting the water in the darkness. The waiter returned with my drink a moment later.

"What time will we arrive in Washington?" I asked.

"Just before seven o'clock in the morning Sir," he reported. "We have half a dozen stops along the route, along with a two hour lay-over in New York City," he explained. I thanked him, and he walked off. I took a sip on the high ball and eased back in the booth.

Twenty minutes passed before she appeared in the Dining Car. She had changed into a more casual outfit, and was wearing a brown angora sweater with a pair of gray pleated slacks. She sat down in the seat directly across from me.

"Hello Mr. Chambers," she said as she took a sip from the gin and tonic.

"Shouldn't you call me Nick, seeing that we're husband and wife?" I held my hand up to show off the gold ring.

"Please take good care of that," she advised. "I'm actually getting married in three weeks and my fiancée would be devastated if anything should happen to it."

"Just who are you anyway?" I asked as I pulled my smokes out and offered her one. She slid one from the pack, and I lit a match to it for her. She paused and glanced out the window at the passing landscape.

"I'm sure you remember Agent Valentine?" she questioned. I nodded to let her know that I did. "Well he's Director Valentine now and he happened to read about your secretary's death in the paper on Monday afternoon. My name is agent Burroughs, Evelyn Burroughs. I work for the Director and he asked that I look into the matter for him."

"How did you happen to find me?" I questioned. She laughed and took a slow drag on her cigarette.

"That was actually a bit of dumb luck," she confessed. "Well... I went downtown and interviewed some of the detectives investigating your secretary's murder. I had a chance to speak with your friend Detective Bradley while I was there, and he reluctantly told me that you had asked him to run a plate on a car belonging to the Belarus Embassy in Washington, D.C. That interested me... It interested me very much Nick." She lifted her head and stared at me across the table. She had beautiful soft chestnut eyes that a man could get lost in. "Well... I put two and two together and had a hunch you might head south. It was sheer luck I noticed you sleeping in the station while I was waiting for the overnight train."

"What's with the marriage gag?" I asked.

"I saw that the police were checking all passengers who were boarding and knew you wouldn't make it through on your own. I actually just picked up the rings this morning at our jeweler. I had to think quickly and it was simply the first thing that came to my mind," she explained. I blew some smoke in her direction and took a sip off the highball. The waiter came back to our table.

"Are you ready to order?" he asked.

"I am," she replied. "I'm starving. I'll have the sirloin, cooked medium, with some mashed potatoes and green beans." The waiter wrote her order down and looked at me.

"I'll have the same, only burn the steak." He nodded and walked off. I looked across the table at her. "Does that mean the Providence Police are investigating the embassy?" I questioned.

"No," she answered. "They seem convinced that you killed your secretary Nick, and a judge has already issued a warrant for your arrest."

"And what do you believe?" I asked.

"Let's just say the FBI is more open-minded," she replied. "The Director trusts you and believes there may be more to Bridgette's murder than a simple lover's spat, or whatever convenient motive the local authorities are attributing this to."

"How does the Belarus embassy fit in?' I asked. She glanced out at the darkness again, hesitant to tell me more than I needed to know.

"How did you happen to come across that license plate Nick?" she questioned back.

"A newsy saw a man leaving my office building early on Monday morning right around the time of Bridgette's murder. He got into a black Packard with diplomatic plates," I explained.

"Did he get a description?" she asked hopefully.

"He did, and I was able to run down a name," I replied. She leaned closer across the table as if to tell me to whisper the name quietly to her. I leaned in close to her, close enough to smell the French perfume on her pale neck. "What does the Belarus embassy have to do with all of this?" I asked for the second time. She leaned back in her seat.

"If we're going to work together Nick, you'll need to tell me everything you know," she advised.

"I could say the same to you," I answered. She bit her lip in frustration and gazed out the window for a moment considering the stalemate.

"Much of what I know is classified Nick, and I'm simply not at liberty to talk about it. If you could tell me this man's name, it might help to tie things together, and I might be able to help put some of the pieces in place for you," she suggested. "If you tell me nothing we're simply at an impasse. I would think you would be a little grateful that I stuck my neck out for you back there," she said batting her soft eyes at me now.

"It's not that I don't appreciate what you did for me," I said. "Putting our marriage aside for the moment, we only just met, and I haven't completely decided if I should trust you." She pulled a gold federal buzzer out from her purse and laid it down on the table for me to admire.

"I'm a federal agent Nick. I could call the conductor over right now and have you put under house arrest. The fact that I haven't done so should say something," she suggested.

"It does say something. I'm just not exactly sure what yet," I replied, staring back into her eyes. I stewed for a moment and drank more scotch before finally relenting. "His name is Isaac Demidov. I was able to track him down to the Turks Head Club in Providence." I paused. "Alright, you got your name, now how does the Belarus embassy fit in?" I pressed. She smiled back at me and took another sip on her drink.

"I'm glad we're trusting one another Nick. Isaac Demidov is a well-known diplomat from the Republic of Belarus," she explained. "You believe that he murdered your secretary?"

"I'll let you know once I ask him?" I replied. She smiled again and took a long drag on her cigarette.

"It wouldn't matter if he did. He has diplomatic immunity. The police wouldn't be able to convict him or even arrest him for that matter," she explained.

"I don't plan on doing either of those things," I replied. She looked up at me, somewhat surprised.

"I see," she commented. A concerned expression ran down her face.

"How do you know so much about this Demidov character anyway?" I asked. She glanced over her shoulder at the waiter who was returning with our dinner. He was pushing a small cart with two covered plates.

"Let's save that for the moment Nick, and just enjoy our dinner together. We have a long night ahead of us," she noted. The waiter placed both plates down on the table and uncovered them. The steak looked damn good, so I relented and cut into the sirloin.

When we had finished our dinner, the waiter cleared the table and brought us a fresh set of drinks. The car had cleared by this time and I looked down at my watch. It was eight-thirty.

"So, let's talk some more about Isaac Demidov," I suggested. She shook her head back at me.

"First let's talk more about you Nick," she replied. "I'm curious how you first met Director Valentine?"

"You could say he helped me out of a jam I was in a few years back, and I did a favor for him in return a year or so later." My answer didn't appear to satisfy her, but she moved on.

"He seems to trust you for some reason Nick," she commented. I lit two fresh cigarettes and handed one over to her. "I saw the package that you mailed to your detective friend," she added.

"Is that so," I replied. "Someone left that little item in my ice box, then placed a call to the cops to come and search my place. Do the police think it came from me?"

"I'm afraid so Nick," she replied. "They traced it back to the post office at Lindsey's Market. That, along with the two eyewitnesses who saw you leaving the building Monday morning was all the judge needed to issue an arrest warrant," she explained. "Your friend Tom did his best to talk them out of it, but I'm afraid the Lieutenant seems convinced of your guilt. I had an opportunity to speak with the Lieutenant and he told me that he wasn't surprised at all, that he knew your type and knew you would… Well, how did he put it, go off the rails someday."

"Two eye witnesses that nobody ever saw or heard of before. Ten to one they would never show up in court to testify against me, but by then it wouldn't really matter. Especially if they had found that knife in my ice box."

"I agree Nick. On the surface it appears that someone has gone to a great deal of trouble to shift guilt in your direction," she observed.

"Yeah… Well, I'm nobody's patsy lady. I'll find this Isaac character and when I do, I'll beat a confession out of him."

"You can't be sure that he was even involved Nick," she commented. "It's entirely possible that he had business in your building on Monday morning and just happened to be leaving around the time Bridgette was killed. Keep in mind that he's a well-respected diplomat, with several banking interests in the northeast. I couldn't begin to imagine the political connections he may have. But even if he were responsible, based on what you've told me, don't you think he would have an alibi planned for himself? Perhaps a tenant in the building that would testify he was meeting with Demidov that morning."

"What if he does?" I shot back. "That type of thing won't make any difference to me. I'll beat the truth out of him, and I'll do it front of you so you can witness the confession, and when I'm done he's getting two slugs in the belly. Then I'll watch him die slowly, just as he watched Bridgette die."

"The FPI doesn't work that way Nick," she replied.

"Well Nick Chambers does sweetheart! If you don't have the stomach for it you can get off at the next stop, no hard feelings. A credible witness would be preferable, but either way I'll get by."

"Beating confessions out of people won't hold up in court Nick," she added.

"It works for the cops all the time. But if they still hang this rap on me, at least I'll have a clean conscious. But let's be clear about one thing sister, whoever killed Bridgette isn't getting his day in court," I stated.

"I can't be any part of that Nick," she replied calmly.

"And just how do you know so much about Isaac Demidov," I questioned. She blew some smoke from her lungs and leaned closer to me across the table. Her eyes had dropped slightly. The gin had started to do its work.

"He's a foreign diplomat Nick, and the FBI keeps tabs on all foreign diplomats. Besides, you might say he's a person of interest to the bureau," she added.

"Interest in what way?" I asked.

"That's the confidential part. But you might say your circumstance doesn't seem so unbelievable to us, and we're very interested in learning more about Mr. Demidov and his organization."

"Organization?" I questioned. She lifted her head and opened her eyes wide now.

"I think it's time that we got some rest," she suggested. "Tomorrow is likely to be a busy day for both of us." She stood up without waiting for a response and began walking towards the front of the car. I threw some cash on the table for the waiter and followed close behind.

As we approached the door, a broad shouldered rough looking young man stepped inside the dining car and passed by Evelyn. As he passed me his shoulder collided with mine. I turned back quickly to look at him and noticed a smile fading from his face, then he spoke up.

"Sorry mister," he muttered unpersuasively. I said nothing and kept walking. We passed through several coach cars with weary looking passengers tossing uncomfortably in their seats. When we reached the sleeping car, Evelyn used a small brass key to open the last door on the left.

It was a small sleeper cabin, with a large window looking out at the passing darkness. There was sleeper couch against one wall, with a pull-down bed just above it. The car had a single shared bathroom out in the hallway. The heavy suitcase I had helped to carry on board was lying on the couch now. She opened it and pulled a pair of pajamas out from inside.

"I'll run out and use the bathroom first if it's ok with you Nick?" she asked.

I nodded and she went out, closing the door as she exited. I looked down at the large open suitcase and made a quick decision to search it. I gently lifted the neatly folded clothes on top and placed them down on the lower bed, then opened a second compartment below the clothes.

My eyes must have bugged out of their sockets as I examined the contents. There was a wad of cash rolled up neatly at the bottom of the case. I lifted and thumbed through the thick roll, counting the bills. It had to be close to five hundred dollars in assorted bills. There were several passports, all with Evelyn's photo, but none with the name she had given me. Most interesting was a cache of weapons, which included several folding pocket knives, a Colt .45 automatic, a .32 Walther PPK, and a compact Beretta .38 semi-automatic with holster. There were six boxes of ammunition packed at the bottom of the suitcase.

It suddenly hit me that I had left my gun in the station locker back in New London. This seemed like quite a store of ammunition for a lone FBI agent, and I was starting to feel a bit inadequate. I opened one of the ammo boxes and loaded seven rounds into the Beretta magazine, then snapped the clip into the small gun. I tucked it away in the leather holster and took one of the small folding knives for good measure. I stashed them both in my jacket pocket and hung the leather coat up on the wall hook, then closed the flap inside the suitcase and placed Evelyn's clothes neatly back on top. I cracked the window an inch and sat back down on the couch, then set fire to a fresh cigarette. She retuned ten minutes later dressed in her pajamas with her hair up in a net.

"It's all yours," she remarked. "If it's all right with you I'll take the top bunk."

"Separate beds on our honeymoon?" I questioned. She just rolled her eyes at me and climbed up top.

I picked up the small overnight bag which I had purchased in New London, then walked outside to the restroom. I turned the tap on and splashed some water on my tired face, then brushed my teeth. I hadn't brought any overnight clothes to change into, so I headed back to the cabin. When I got there, Evelyn was already under the covers in the top bunk. Some soft snoring told me she was sleeping. The gin and tonic had apparently taken a toll on her. I couldn't help but be disappointed, considering it was my first honeymoon.

I sat on the lower couch and took my shoes off, rubbed my tired feet, and eased back down in the makeshift bed to get some rest. I had trouble sleeping and was still half awake two hours later when I heard a scratching sound coming from outside of our cabin. I stood up and walked over to the door. I put my ear up against the wood and listened. The sound was coming from the brass lock. There was something scratching inside of it. Someone was trying to pick the lock from the outside.

I stepped back and reached over in the darkness to my jacket hanging on the wall. I felt inside the pocket for the Beretta, but it was gone. Never trust a woman I thought to myself, but she had at least left the knife for me. I took it out and unfolded the blade. The scratching on the door suddenly stopped. I stood there in silence for a moment, listening intently. An eternity passed without sound, but then it came, footsteps hurrying away outside. I rushed to the door and opened it. As I stepped into the narrow hallway, the door at the back of the car swung shut. I folded the blade and put it away my pocket, then began walking briskly towards the rear of the train.

I passed through two coach cars with passengers half-asleep in their seats. An elderly woman sat up reading a book under a night lamp.

"Excuse me Ma-am, did someone just pass thorough this car?" I whispered. She nodded and pointed to the rear of the car.

"He went straight through," she replied with some annoyance, pointing to the rear door. I nodded and headed back into the next car. This time I saw him, just as he was exiting. He turned for a split second and glanced back at me before going into the dining car. It was the same young man who had bumped into me earlier.

I walked quickly through the last coach, passed through a set of doors and stepped into the dining car. The car was darkened and completely empty now. Tables had already been set for tomorrow morning's breakfast. I noticed the door at the rear of the car was cracked open. I walked through car slowly checking under each of the tables, but the place appeared to be empty. I opened the door at the end and stepped cautiously out onto a small rear observation platform. It was empty.

"I turned instinctually and looked back inside of the car, but it was still empty. The platform was no more than four feet wide by a few feet deep, and he clearly wasn't on it. It might have been possible for him to jump, but the train was moving at a good clip now, maybe forty or fifty miles per hour, and it wouldn't be a risk-free jump. I looked around the corner towards the front of the train and noticed an iron ladder bolted to the side that led up top. There was a swing gate on the side of the platform that I opened. I reached around and grabbed a hold of the ladder and started up. As I left the protection of the rear platform, a heavy gust of wind pushed up against me, trying to slow my progress. I hugged the side and climbed, eventually reaching the top.

He was there, belly climbing across the roof of the dining car. He had already made it about half the distance across. I stood up into a crouched position and started running at him. He turned and saw me advancing on him, stood up himself and began running for the next car.

Forward progress was like running against a heavy gust in a hurricane. He reached the connection to the next car and jumped over. A moment later I reached the same gap between cars and looked across. It was about a four-foot span, but against a heavy wind. I took a few steps back and made a run at it.

I made the jump but landed hard and slid off to the right side of the train. There was a guard rail on the side that I grabbed a hold of, saving me from a treacherous fall. I hung there dangling like a bug on a windshield for a minute, but finally found my footing and slowly climbed back up. When I reached the top, I was completely exhausted and laid there flat on my stomach for a moment. My interest in chasing this punk had suddenly evaporated.

Before I could even turn over, I felt a hand grab at the back of my hair and yank my head up. Suddenly there was something around my neck and squeezing hard. I reached both hands under the heavy cord that was closing tightly around my throat and tried to block its progress. I struggled to my knees and fought against the heavy force choking my breath away, but knew I was losing the battle. I only had seconds before I would pass out.

I reached one hand into my pocket, pulled the knife out, and flicked the blade open with my thumb. I was starting to get light headed now and used whatever strength I had left to sink the blade into his upper thigh, then pulled it quickly out. The rope slackened almost immediately, and I turned to face him.

He was clutching at the fresh wound in his thigh. His face reddened suddenly, and he rushed at me. I thrust the small blade into his throat and he reeled backwards. He straightened up suddenly, pulling the knife out from the side of his neck. Blood sprayed from his jugular like a leaky hose. He staggered for a minute, trying to shake off the lethal wound, then lost his balance and disappeared over the side into the darkness.

I collapsed down on the roof and fought to get my breath back. After a few minutes, I felt the train slowing and looked up. We were approaching a station on the right, about a half mile away. I got up and started back, jumped across to the dining car and ran crouched to the end of the train. I lowered myself down the ladder to the observation platform and headed back inside.

I walked calmly back through each of the cars. All of the passengers seemed to be peacefully sleeping now, unaware of the life and death struggle that had just taken place above their heads. I opened the door to our cabin. Evelyn rolled over in her bed half-asleep.

"That was a long time in the bathroom?" she remarked in a drowsy voice before turning back over and dozing off again. I sat down on the lower bed and took in some deep breaths for a moment, before lying down and closing my eyes.

Seventeen: A Visit to our Nation's Capitol:

An announcement echoed over the train's loud speaker system.

"The train will be arriving in Washington D.C. in one hour. All passengers must depart, this is our final destination."

I sat up in bed and rubbed my bloodshot eyes, then stood up to see if Evelyn was still sleeping. To my surprise the top bunk was empty, and the bed had already been made. I looked around the small cabin and noticed her suitcase was gone. I was just about to check outside, when I noticed a scrap of paper stuck to the cabin mirror. I lifted the folded paper and read the handwritten note.

Meet you in the dining car, Evelyn

I put my shoes on, grabbed my overnight bag, and headed outside. I made a quick pitstop in the restroom to clean up, then started for the back of the train.

The coach cars that had been fast asleep the night before were awake and alive with activity now, as passengers readied for departure. When I entered the dining car, I caught sight of her right away. She was seated in the same booth from the night before, with her back up against the rear wall. She was facing forward and waved to me as soon as I entered. Her suitcase was seated beside her. She was dressed more casually than a day earlier, and her bare legs were stretched out beneath the table. They were nice legs that I hadn't had a chance to notice up until now. I sat down in the seat across from her. She was smoking a cigarette and drinking a cup of black coffee.

"I was just about to send the steward out to find you Nick," she greeted. I poured myself a cup of coffee from the carafe on the table and lit a smoke. "How did you sleep?" she asked.

"Like a baby," I reported.

"We'll need to think about transportation once we get to the station," she commented. Inside my head I was still debating whether Evelyn could help me in Washington, or if I would be better off on my own. She had access to resources that I didn't have, but I wasn't looking to attract attention to myself, and when the time came to get justice for Bridgette, she might get in my way. I had to find out if she had already notified anyone about me.

"Did you arrange for a car?" I asked. She nodded.

"No, but I can make a call as soon as we reach the station," she replied.

"I think things might go better if we kept our whereabouts to ourselves for the time being," I suggested. "The less people that know the better. I've got some cash and we can rent a car when we get there."

"I'll need to update the Director on my status Nick," she replied.

"Listen Evelyn, I don't have all the answers yet, but I do know this thing is far reaching. Whoever killed Bridgette has connections. They've moved too fast with witnesses and warrants for this not to involve someone with political connections at a very high level. I don't want anyone knowing we're in D.C. until we're fifty miles out. It's just better that way. Otherwise someone is likely to throw a net over us the moment we walk through Union Station." She took a deep drag on her cigarette and gazed out through the window at the passing green fields of Maryland.

"Alright Nick," she agreed. "I still have to report in when we get there, otherwise it would only set off alarms back at the bureau, but I won't say that I've found you yet. Will that do?" she offered. I wasn't crazy about it, but I didn't have much choice. I had to trust her.

"Ok," I replied. "We'll find a cab somewhere away from the station. They may have already alerted the rental companies." She nodded in agreement. The waiter came by and we ordered a light breakfast. We felt the train slowing just as we were paying our bill.

"If there is anyone in the station Nick, they'll be looking for a single middle-aged man. Let's keep up the honeymoon act. I think it's our best bet," she advised.

"I'm not sure I like the middle-aged crack, but I'll play along," I replied. The train staggered to a stop and a whistle blew somewhere outside.

We got up and walked to the forward cars where passengers were departing. People young and old were stepping down onto the station platform with heavy luggage in tow. Porters were standing on the deck ready to assist needy passengers with their items. Business men and politicians stepped off at a brisk pace with their brief cases on their way into work. Evelyn and I were among the last people to step off the train. One of the porters approached us but I waved him off. The luggage helped to give the appearance of a couple traveling on vacation. Subtle things mattered and would be noticed by a plain clothes detective on the lookout.

We passed through a set of large doors into Union Station with its high gilded arched ceilings. Rows of wooden benches lined polished granite floors of vast open space. I carried her luggage in one hand and held her hand with the other. Married life wasn't easy I thought to myself. We began walking through the crowded station, and I started eyeballing the place for law enforcement. Evelyn instinctually did the same.

"See anything," she whispered.

"Yeah... Four rows down on the left, sitting with the newspaper in front of his face," I replied. She shifted her gaze onto a tall man seated in a trench coat several rows away. "Just keep walking," I advised. She stopped suddenly in her tracks and took the luggage from me, then opened the case in the middle of the station floor. She pretended to search through it for a moment, then snapped it shut and straightened up with a look of frustration on her face. It had caught the man's attention and he placed the paper down on his lap to watch us now.

"You forgot to pack the camera Bob!" she yelled at me in an exasperated voice. "What are we going to do now?" she added. "How could you leave our camera at home on a trip to Washington, D.C.?" she asked contemptuously. She was good. You would have thought we'd been married twenty years. I did what most husbands do and said nothing. She shook her head, lifted the luggage up and walked away from me in disgust. I saw a smile pass across the detective's face as he picked up the paper and went back to his reading. I put my tail between my legs and followed close behind her.

We passed through a set of entrance doors and walked out under an enormous portico filled with cabs and buses. We walked a block or two away from the station before hailing a taxi. The driver was an old timer with thin grey hair and a two-day stubble covering his face. An unlit cigar hung trapped between his teeth.

"Where to folks?" he asked without removing the dead cigar from his mouth. Evelyn and I looked at each other. We had been in such a hurry to get through the station, we hadn't thought through our next move.

"We're on a one-night layover. Can you recommend any good hotels, maybe close to the embassy district?" I asked.

"There's the Carlyle Hotel on New Hampshire, near Dupont Circle?" he suggested looking through his rear-view mirror.

"Sounds perfect, thanks," I replied. He put the taxi into gear and drove off.

We drove down Massachusetts Ave in the direction of Dupont Circle. I could see the Washington Monument standing high off in the distance. When we reached Dupont Circle, he turned right onto New Hampshire Avenue. The place was loaded with townhouses and Embassy's. We passed by one building in particular that caught my attention, the Embassy of the Republic of Belarus. The Carlyle Hotel was located a couple of blocks after it on the right. The driver pulled up to the curb and got out to help us with our luggage. I paid him the fare, tipped him, and we went inside.

The floor inside the front lobby was made of black and white Italian marble, the lights and stainless stair rails had art deco lines. A set of black marble stairs led up to a second level. The reception desk was off to the left as we walked inside. The middle-aged man standing behind the front desk was tall and well dressed. He wore a gray pinstriped suit with a dark navy tie over a pressed white shirt. A set of reading glasses rested on the tip of his roman nose as he looked across the reception desk at us.

"Good morning, how may I help you?" he questioned.

"Where looking for a room, most likely just for one night, but possibly two?" I answered.

"Do you have a reservation?" he questioned. I shook my head.

"Unfortunately, we don't," Evelyn cut in. "But we would appreciate anything you could do for us," she added as she flashed her golden federal badge over the counter at him. It seemed to have impact and he started to run his thin finger through a large reservation book.

"I can put you up in 814, that's on the top floor," he offered. "Should we bill the bureau?" he questioned to Evelyn.

"No," I interrupted. "We're actually not here on business. Strictly a personal trip." I pulled a twenty out from my wallet and placed it down on the counter. "We'll put a cash deposit down if that's alright," I added.

"Very good Sir," he answered with a smile. "Just sign the guest register and I'll go and get your key."

I flipped the heavy book around and lifted a pen from the counter. I signed us in as Mr. and Mrs. Edward Robinson, room 814, then turned the book back around. A minute later he returned with our room key and handed it to Evelyn, along with a written receipt for the twenty dollars.

"Welcome to the Carlyle Mr. and Mrs. Robinson. If you wouldn't mind giving us a few minutes to ready the room. You can leave your luggage here at the desk and I'll have the porter bring it up when the room is ready," he explained.

"We'd like to rent a car for the day and do a little sight-seeing. Could you help us with that?" I asked.

"Of course, Mr. Robinson. I'll have one brought over immediately," he replied with crisp efficiency. "There's a bar at the far end of the lobby. Grace can make you a coffee or soda while you're waiting for your room," he suggested. "It should only be fifteen or twenty minutes." I nodded, and we left the luggage with him at the front desk.

We found a large t-shaped bar towards the rear of the lobby, just as he had described. An older woman stood in boredom behind a long mahogany counter. She walked over as soon as we sat down.

"Good morning folks," she greeted pleasantly. She looked to be in her early sixties, red faced and stout, with gray hair pulled back into a tight bun. She wore a burgundy apron with an image of the White House embroidered into it. She placed two napkins down on the counter in front of us. "What can I get you both?" she asked.

"A cup of tea please," Evelyn ordered.

"I'll have coffee, black," I added. The old woman nodded and walked back through a door at the rear of the bar. I pulled out my smokes and lit two, then handed one over to Evelyn. She took in a deep drag, propped her head up with her hand and looked over at me.

"So, what's our next move Nick?" she questioned.

"We stake out that embassy and see if our friend shows up," I said.

"How do you know he's going to show up?" she asked.

"I don't, but I have reason to believe that Isaac Demidov is in Washington, D.C., and that Embassy is the only connection I have to him. The waitress came back with our drinks and set them down on the counter. I took a sip from the coffee and we waited. Ten minutes passed before the hotel concierge came over to let us know our room was ready. He also handed me a set of keys to a rental car parked out front. He was apparently very efficient.

"I added the rental charge to your room bill Mr. Robinson?" he reported. "The car is parked out in front by the curb. It's a black Ford," he explained. "When you've finished sightseeing, you can bring it back to the front of the hotel and the valet will park it for you." I thanked him and placed a dollar in his hand, then he walked back to his station at the front desk.

"Why don't you go upstairs and check out our room. I'll park the car over near that Embassy and stake it out for a while. It would just be boring work, and I can call you if he shows up," I suggested.

"Nothing doing Nick," she shot back. "If you think I'm letting you out of my sight for one minute, you've got another thing coming. Besides, you just told the hotel concierge we were both going sight-seeing. If you leave by your-self it won't look right." I rubbed the tension from my forehead.

"Alright... We'd better get going then," I relented. The bartender saw us standing up and came over. "Just charge it to room 814," I instructed. She smiled, then nodded to us.

Eighteen: The Belarus Embassy

As promised, the rental car was parked out by the front curb. I started to open the driver's side door, but Evelyn nudged me aside and slid behind the steering wheel.

"It makes more sense for me to drive Nick. After all, I know this town much better than you, and these one-way streets will just get you into trouble." she suggested. I thought it over for a second, then dropped the keys in her lap and walked around the back of the car to the passenger side. She started the engine and we drove off.

The Belarus embassy was just a few blocks away. We drove past it at first and I got a good look at the place, then she drove around Dupont Circle, doubled back down the block and found a spot diagonally across the street. It was a three-story townhouse with a dreary stone façade. A small portico hung over a steep set of front steps. As far as embassies went, it wasn't much to talk about. Evelyn shut the engine down, I cracked my window and lit a smoke, then tried to get comfortable. We sat and watched.

Several uneventful hours passed. A kid flew by on a bike and tossed the morning paper halfway up the front steps, a postman delivered some mail to a box hanging at the base of the stairs, and a young woman dressed as though she might work in the kitchen arrived and went inside. Some more time passed and a policeman on horseback trotted by us. He glanced down as he passed, but kept to his morning rounds. When lunchtime arrived, I got out to stretch my legs and bought a couple of hot dogs from a vendor up the street. Another hour passed with no one entering or leaving the building.

"What if he doesn't show up today?" Evelyn asked as she reached inside the pack of smokes on the seat and drew one out.

"Then we'll come back tomorrow," I answered. I struck a match and lit her cigarette. The cop on horseback was coming back up the road now. I nudged Evelyn to be sure she saw him. He rode up and pulled back on the reins when he reached Evelyn's open window. The horse had a set of tired black eyes that looked back at the officer as if to question what the hold-up was. He leaned down and peered into the sedan at the two of us.

"You folks having car trouble," he asked. "You've been parked here for most of the day." Evelyn instinctually pulled out her wallet and flashed her golden badge at him.

"On the job officer," she replied. He took the badge and looked it over, then handed it back to her.

"Well what do you know, a female Fed," he mumbled to himself. "Anything I can help with?" he offered. I leaned over in the seat.

"You can help by moving along officer, and not attracting any more attention to us," I said in my most authoritative voice. He grunted, tapped the horse with his foot, and they trotted on.

A few more hours passed. It was a little after four o'clock before we caught a break. A car drove up to the curb directly in front of the Embassy and parked. It was a shiny black Packard One-Twenty. It had a beautiful chromium front grill, with polished chromium hubs and silver lines over the bulging wheel wells. She was a beauty and perfectly fit the description that Liam had given me. This was it.

The driver stepped out of the car and looked up and down the street suspiciously. He was a tall lanky man of maybe six feet. He wore a long gray wool overcoat with a chauffeur's hat on his bony head. He headed straight up the stairs and rang the bell aside of the door. A moment later the young woman who had entered the building earlier opened the door and let him inside.

I stepped out from the sedan and crossed the street, then approached the Packard and looked inside the rear window. The back seat was empty. I walked around to the rear of the vehicle and checked the license plate, *Foreign Govt. 314.* It was the same car that Liam had spotted outside of my office on Monday morning, but the chauffeur wasn't the man that Bridgette or Liam had described. I looked across the street and saw Evelyn watching me intently. I looked up at the townhouse and saw that the front door was still shut. I wasn't sure how much time I had before the driver came back out, but I knew I needed to find the man who owned this car... I needed to find Isaac Demidov. I made a quick decision and popped the back trunk open, climbed inside and shut it.

A few minutes passed before I heard the front door on the townhouse open, a door slammed shut, then heavy footsteps coming down the slate stairway. If I was lucky, he had come by to pick up his boss, which meant payback was close at hand. I sat quietly and listened, but only one of the car's doors opened and shut. The engine started, and we were moving.

I knew that Evelyn would tail him as she had been trained to do. We drove for what had to be a few miles, making turns here and there, and disorienting me in the process. At some point the car stopped and I felt the driver rev the engine, then it came. He threw the transmission back into gear and the wheels screeched as the car gunned forward. I rolled backwards hitting my head on the inside of the trunk. I could feel the road passing by violently below me now. He took a half-dozen sharp turns in different directions, riding the curb on most of them. My body slammed up against the trunks interior as I held on to whatever I could. A minute later the car slowed and rolled to a halt.

The engine stopped, and I heard him exit the vehicle. I listened to the sound of footsteps fading away towards the rear of the car, then cracked the trunk open an inch. He was already thirty yards away, walking down the sidewalk at a brisk pace. He mustn't have realized I was inside. Evelyn had tailed us, but he had spotted her. Now he was ditching the car and escaping on foot.

I climbed out from the trunk and looked around. The black sedan we had rented was nowhere in sight, and neither was Evelyn. He had given her the slip. I stepped up onto the sidewalk and began calmly tailing him on foot.

Nineteen: Washington Monument

Once my eyes had adjusted to the sunlight, I realized where we were. He had parked along the National Mall and we were walking in the direction of the Washington Monument. I let him get fifty yards out in front of me. Tourists gradually filled the gap between us, but I was still able to keep a bead on him. He looked back nervously over his shoulder once or twice, but I was certain he hadn't noticed me yet.

He finally made his way up the hill to the towering monument. There was a park ranger and small group of tourists there getting ready to go up. He mixed in with the group, then walked inside with them. I sat down on a stone bench outside, pulled out a smoke and waited.

Forty minutes passed before the group of tourists emerged from the base of the monument. I scanned each person as they exited. The last people to come out, just before the park ranger, were a couple and their young son. The boy looked to be about five years old. I waited a few more minutes as the crowd disbursed, but the man I had tailed never came out.

I tossed my cigarette onto the ground and started up the mound to the base of the monument. The ranger was still standing there making his notes on a small steno pad when I approached.

"Sorry mister, the last tour of the day just came down," he explained. He was an older man in his early sixties, a little over five feet in height, thin with gray fading hair and a thick set of eye glasses. I looked up at the high stone monument. It seemed even taller up close.

"We took our young son up earlier, and I think he left his favorite cap up top," I explained. "He's balling his eyes out back at the hotel. Would you mind if we ran up quickly to look for it?" I asked. He looked tired and glanced up at the lofty structure, daunted by the thought of one more trip to the top.

"All right mister… I wouldn't want your youngster crying all night, but if you don't mind going up by yourself. I've been up five times already today and these knees just aren't what they used to be. Run up and have a look," he instructed.

"Thanks," I said as he held the door open for me.

I stepped inside and took a quick look around the place.

Hanging on the stone walls were historical photos of the monument being built towards the end of the nineteenth century, along with dedication plaques to Washington and other dignitaries of the time. The first floor seemed completely empty. I followed the tour guide ropes to a spiral staircase that led up to the top. Looking up at the twisted staircase only made me dizzy, but I took a deep breath and started. If he was up there, I knew I would be exhausted by the time I reached him. I needed to pace myself and conserve enough energy to take him on when I got up top. He wasn't going anywhere, and I was going to find out where his boss was.

I hit the two-hundred foot mark and was feeling pretty winded, so I slowed my pace and took my time on the second half. At times I glanced down and saw just how far I had come. The downward spiral seemed endless now and was dizzying to look at. I kept my focus on the steps in front of me and made steady progress. At the four-hundred foot mark I could see an end in sight. I stopped for a moment, allowing time for my breath to recover, then made the final push.

When I reached the observation deck, my eyes fixed immediately on a man standing directly in front of the lookout window. It was the chauffeur. He was gazing out the window back in the direction of where he had left the Packard, probably trying to see if anyone was watching it. He was startled by my arrival and glanced back at me for a moment, but then turned his attention back outside down on the ground. I leaned up against one of the walls and set fire to a smoke.

"Last tour left thirty minutes ago pal," I stated calmly. He turned to look me up and down, then faced back out the window without responding.

"You deaf or something?" I asked. "I said the last tour already ended a half an hour ago." He turned back at me.

"I stay a little longer," he muttered in some foreign accent I didn't care to recognize, although it sounded similar to the one the dentist had spoken with.

"That's fine with me pal," I replied. "I'd just as soon ask you what I need to know up here."

"I not meet you before," he shot back at me. "I no talk to you mista," he said without turning around.

"Oh, you're gonna talk to me. When I'm done with you, you'll be talking silly pal," I explained. He turned around slowly, giving me a second look.

"How do you Americans say… Beat it!" he spouted, turning to face me straight on now. I smiled at him and took a long drag on my smoke.

"You're gonna tell me where your boss is at," I said. "This can go the hard way or the easy way, but in the end, you're going to talk to me."

"I tell you nothing," he spewed back at me, while drawing a switchblade out of his pocket. He pushed a button and the stainless-steel blade flicked open.

"That won't change anything pal," I noted, dragging calmly on my smoke. "It only means we're going do things the hard way, but you'll still spill the beans in the end," I said confidently. "Where's Demidov?" I questioned.

His face painted red and he lunged at me with his knife. I side-stepped the attack, grabbed his knife hand with my left and struck hard at his throat with my right fist. He felt it and the knife dropped to the ground. He regained his composure quickly and came at me again. This time he caught me with a right to the side of my face. I took it and swung an upper cut to his jaw. Teeth cracked somewhere inside of his mouth. I followed up quickly with a left hook to the side of his head. His knees buckled, and he fell hard to the ground.

He made a desperate reach for the blade on the floor, but I stomped on his bare hand with my heel, then grabbed his head by the hair and slammed it back down into the iron floor.

He was dazed now and lying on his stomach. I pulled his head up and crouched down to speak with him face to face.

"It's only going to get worse from here pal," I explained. "Just tell me where your boss is at, and you might walk away without a trip to the hospital." He looked up at me and spit in my face. I dragged him up by his shoulders and threw him head first into the iron railing. He staggered back to his feet, then looked desperately around the place for someone to come to his aid. No one would. He was panting and visibly sweating now. Blood ran down the side of his forehead.

"I tell you nothing!" he shouted just before jumping over the rail and dropping down out of sight. I ran to the railing just in time to see his body ping-ponging up against the steel railing on its way down to the bottom. He faded out of sight, but I eventually heard a thud that echoed up through the staircase when he hit bottom. I stood there dumbfounded for a moment, shook my head and started back down.

I double-timed it on my way down and made it to the bottom in short order. Whatever was left of him was seeping into the cement floor. I reached into his jacket pocket, pulled the keys to the Packard out, then straightened myself up and went back outside. The park ranger was still there waiting for me, smoking a cigar. He had a round key ring hanging from his hip.

"Find the boys cap?" he asked hopefully. I shook my head.

"No dice… He must have dropped it at the Lincoln Memorial. I'll head over there now," I answered.

"What happened to your eye?" he questioned while examining my face. I touched at my swollen cheek.

"I took a fall on the stairway coming down," I explained.

"I thought I heard something," he commented. "I got a first aid kit inside if you need it?" he offered.

"I'll be fine," I answered. "Thanks for your help."

He fingered through his key ring, picked one out and put it into the brass lock on the door to secure it. I shook his hand, turned and walked off. It would be a grisly discovery for the park ranger on duty the following morning. Chalk up another murder rap for Chambers, I thought to myself. The bodies were piling up and too many witnesses to place me at the scene. I had to find Demidov before the police caught up with me.

I doubled back to the Packard and searched the car twice but came up empty, then started the engine and drove away. On the way back to the hotel, I noticed a three-story parking garage and had an idea. As I pulled into the lot, a young attendant approached my window.

"Long-term or short-term mister? He asked.

"Long term," I replied. He tucked a blue tag under my wiper and pointed upstairs.

"Take it up to the second floor," he instructed. I nodded and drove into the garage. I followed the driveway up one level and found an empty spot. I stepped out from the car and looked around the place. There was an Oldsmobile a few cars down with a blue tag under its wiper. The car had a thin film of pollen on it, which told me it had been parked there for some time.

I walked to the rear of the car and crouched down by the plate. It was a Virginia license. I used a dime to loosen the screws and made quick work removing both plates, then replaced the diplomatic plates on the Packard with the stolen Virginia ones. I tossed the diplomatic plates into a trash can, got back inside the Packard and drove back down. The attendant shot a puzzled look at me as I came out.

"Forgot my luggage," I explained. "I need to run back to the house." He nodded and waved me on.

Darkness was just setting in as I pulled up to the curb at the Carlyle. A young Mex who was valeting cars walked out from under the portico and opened my door for me. I left the engine running and handed the kid a buck.

"Room 814," I told him as I walked inside.

Twenty: Midnight Excursion

When I opened the door to our room, Evelyn was lying on a king-sized bed. She had fallen asleep on top of the covers, still dressed as she had been earlier. Her shoes had been tossed to the ground and her bare legs were staring coolly back it me. They were beautiful legs that caught my attention and raised my blood pressure a few points. I closed the door and took my jacket off. She heard me and rose up from her sleep.

"Nick!" she exclaimed as she jumped up from the bed. She ran to me and wrapped her arms around me. I felt her warm full body press up against mine. She stepped back and looked at my swollen eye. "What happened to your face?" she asked.

"It turned out our boy had a pretty decent right cross," I answered.

"What happened to him?" she questioned. "Did you find Demidov?" I shook my head in defeat.

"The chauffeur wouldn't talk," I explained. "After he lost you, he ditched the car and felt like doing some sight-seeing, so I followed him on foot. I cornered him at the top of the Washington Monument and gave him a pretty good beat down, but he was loyal and wouldn't spill anything about his boss."

"Where is he now?" she asked.

"He's dead… Took a swan dive over the rail and landed five hundred feet below," I explained.

"Nick… You didn't?" she asked tentatively.

"I didn't," I answered. "Just some kind of sick loyalty to his boss I suppose."

"Well, where do we go from here?" she asked.

"I'm going to take a shower and get in a few hours shut eye," I replied. "Then you and I are going to break into the Belarus Embassy later tonight." Her face went deadpan. She thought it over for a moment, then her pretty head nodded in agreement. "How about calling down for some room service and a little scotch?" I asked. She smiled and lifted the receiver on the house phone.

When I came out of the shower, a highball was sitting on the desk in the room waiting for me. Evelyn was sitting at the end of the bed sipping on a gimlet. I drank down some of the scotch and sat on the bed beside her.

"Wake me in a few hours, will you?" I asked. She nodded, and I leaned back in the bed.

"Just how do you plan on breaking into a foreign embassy?" she asked.

"We'll improvise," I answered as my eyes shut and I drifted off.

They opened in what seemed just a few minutes later. Evelyn was sitting on the bed beside me and shaking my shoulder.

"Wake up sleepy head," she coaxed. I rubbed my eyes and looked up at her.

"What time is it?" I asked. "I thought I told you to let me sleep for a few hours." She laughed back at me.

"That hit on your head must have really knocked you for a loop. It's after midnight, and I thought we had plans to start our criminal careers tonight."

"How long have I been out?" I asked.

"Almost five hours," she replied.

"Alright then, let's get going," I said as I got up and put my leather jacket on. "Things might go a little easier if you lend me some of that arsenal your packing in your suitcase," I suggested. Her eyes rolled, and she shot a suspicious look at me.

"Well… At least you're asking this time. What happened to the knife I let you keep?" she asked.

"I left it with someone on the train," I answered. She snickered and walked over to her luggage, released the two side latches, and lifted open the case. She removed some clothing and opened the hidden compartment, then rotated the case for me to view its contents.

"The Beretta should do the job," I said. She reached in and removed it from the retaining clip, then tossed it across the bed at me. She took the Walther PPK for herself and tucked it away in her hand purse. I removed the magazine and checked the ammunition. It still had the shells I had loaded on the train. I snapped the clip back in place and put the gun away in my jacket.

The clerk in the lobby eyed us as we walked past him. We headed out through the large brass front doors and down onto the sidewalk. There was a half-moon hanging gingerly in the midnight sky. I took Evelyn's hand and we strolled down the street as a newly married couple might.

After a few blocks, we approached the Belarus Embassy. The place seemed lifeless, with no lights on at all inside. I took a quick look up and down the street, but the neighborhood seemed deserted. I stooped down and picked up a rock from the gutter, then threw it up at the streetlight directly in front of the building. It was a skill I had acquired as a kid, which came in handy from time to time. The stone hit its target, the bulb popped, and glass dropped down onto the sidewalk. I tugged quickly on Evelyn's hand and pulled her behind a set of tall shrubs just in front of the embassy. We waited for several minutes in the darkness. No one paid any attention to us and the embassy windows remained darkened.

"Can you climb?" I asked. She looked up at the side of the building and nodded. There was a small stone patio over the front door, just outside of a second-floor doorway. We went up the stairs and climbed over to a ledge on one of the first story windows. I boosted Evelyn up on my shoulders and she climbed up onto the small patio. I reached up, grabbed the ledge and pulled myself up and over.

There was a door with an arched window above it that led out onto the small patio. I tried the door, but it was locked. I pulled the Beretta out and was about to smash in one of the glass panes on the door when Evelyn stepped in front of me. She pulled a small leather pouch from her purse and laid it down on the ground, then removed two thin hairpin like instruments. She went to work picking the door lock, snapping it open in under a minute, then put the small burglar's kit away in her purse. We opened the door and stepped into the second-floor hallway.

"You're full of surprises," I whispered to her. "Do they teach you that in FBI school?" I questioned. She rolled her eyes back at me.

"What are we looking for?" she asked.

"Anything that tells us where Isaac Demidov is," I replied. There were four doors off the second-floor hallway, then a stairway leading down to the first level. There was a doorway at the end of the hall close to where we had entered. I opened it and saw a second stairway leading up to a third floor.

"Might as well start at the top and work our way down," I suggested. I pulled my penlight out and switched it on, then started up the darkened stairway.

On the third floor, there were two closed doors at the top of the stairway. We entered the first door, which was a small bedroom with a made twin bed, dresser, and closet. We searched the room but came up empty. It was just a clean empty bedroom that didn't seem to belong to anyone in particular.

We moved on to a second room that was filled with wall-to-wall file cabinets. The labels on the drawers were in a foreign language that meant nothing to me, but Evelyn seemed interested. She pulled a small flashlight of her own from her purse and began opening drawers and searching through files. She was a regular boy scout, always prepared.

"You search up here, I'll take a look down on the second floor," I suggested. She nodded subconsciously as she continued to rifle through the files.

I left the room and went back down to the second floor. The first two doors led into a large meeting room with a rectangular polished table surrounded by thirteen mahogany high-backed chairs. There was a bookshelf built into the outside wall. I passed my light over some of the titles. They were mostly legal books, dozens of thick volumes on state and federal regulations. A large grandfather clock stood alone at one end of the room ticking away a steady beat. There wasn't much else to see.

I went back out into the hallway and opened the third door, which revealed a small washroom and shower. The fourth room had a small brass plate on the door, with some writing I couldn't understand;

Главный дипломат Беларуси.

I started to worry that even if we found something, we wouldn't know what it was.

I opened the door and stepped into a neatly furnished office. There was an over-sized mahogany desk with a black leather chair parked directly behind it. There was a radio next to the desk and a multi-line black telephone on top. More bookcases lined the walls of the office and a small fireplace was situated on the opposite wall across from the desk. Hanging just behind the desk was a large red and green flag that must have been the flag of Belarus. A framed map hung to the right of the flag, which I assumed was a map of the country.

What caught my eye was a glass case hanging on the wall to the left of the flag. Inside the display case were dozens of exotic swords and knives. I put my light on the case and ran it slowly up and down. There was an empty hook where one weapon had been removed from the case. I looked at the weapon just beside the vacant spot. It was an exact duplicate of the dagger I had found in my freezer, the one that had killed Bridgette. I was in the right place alright. I opened the glass case and took down the matching knife, then tucked it away inside of my jacket.

I took a seat behind the large desk and began searching through a set of six small drawers. Most were filled with the usual supplies; paper, pencils and pens, along with some embassy letterhead. The bottom drawer was locked, so I used the knife I had just borrowed to pry it open. The small latch broke easy enough and I pulled the drawer open.

The drawer contained some blank envelopes, a handful of printed postcards, a pad with a list of names, and a small seal, the type used on hot wax to seal envelopes. I took the pad out and read some of the names. It was an impressive list. Four senators, two governors, several wealthy industrialists, union leaders, and one well-known criminal. I folded the list and put it away in my pocket, then lifted out one of the postcards. It was an invitation to a formal dinner. The interesting part was that the invitation was printed in English, and the dinner was being held in Rhode Island.

An Invitation to Dinner
Please join us for a celebration of food and festivities to celebrate the inauguration of our new leader.

On Saturday October 20th, 1945
Chateau Sur Mer
Newport, R.I.

My jaw hung open for nearly a minute. Liam had mentioned a sticker on the Packard with the word *chateau* printed on it. I had been in too much of a rush to even look for it on the Packard early today. I lifted the seal and flashed my light on it. It was a symbol of some sort, reversed on the stamp itself, but one that didn't seem to fit with the Belarus Embassy. There was an ink well on the desk so I dipped the seal lightly into the ink, shook off the excess, and pressed it onto the invitation. A symbol appeared. It was a symbol I had seen once before several years earlier, and one that I recognized now. I stared down at the symbol and replayed the events of the past few days in my head. Things were starting to add up, but I still needed some answers. I tucked the invitation in my pocket and left the office.

As I walked back out into the hallway, I heard the latch on the first-floor entrance door turning, then a door being pushed open downstairs. Two voices were talking now. A man and a woman. They were laughing and speaking in another language. I crouched down and looked through the spindles on the stairway railing.

He was a tall burly man in his late thirties, with short gray hair in a crew cut. He wore a London Fog trench coat. He was not the man that Bridgette had described to me over the telephone. The girl was at least ten years younger with long straight black hair that ran smoothly down over her shoulders. She wasn't wearing a coat and her skirt was cut just above the knees. By this time her blouse was already unbuttoned. She had curves in all the right places, and he was admiring them with his heavy hands. He said something to her and the two started up the wide staircase, stopping every few steps to paw at each other. I backtracked quietly and headed up the stairs to the third floor.

I stopped outside of the file room where I had left Evelyn and listened for their footsteps. A few seconds later I heard them starting up the second staircase for the third floor. Now I knew what the empty bedroom was used for. I stepped inside the file room and closed the door behind me.

Evelyn was still looking through a set of heavy folders. She looked up at me as I entered. I put my index finger to my lips. Her face went deadpan as she froze in place. I switched my pen light off and she followed suit. Within a few seconds there were two voices up in the third-floor hallway. They were making their way to the vacant bedroom, but progress was slow. I heard some moaning and then his belt buckle hit the oak floor somewhere out in the hallway. We waited in silence for a moment, then the bedroom door opened and the sound of two bodies compressing the springs on the small bed. The springs continued to moan along with the man and the woman.

I turned my light back on and pointed it around the small file room. There was a window towards the back of the room, which looked to be our only way out at the moment. I went over and unlocked it, then gently eased the window up, taking care not to be heard by the two occupants in the next room. That would have been hard to do, but I wasn't taking any chances.

It took a few minutes to get the window up fully. I helped Evelyn climb out, then followed closely behind her. We were standing on a small semi-circle roof that protruded out from the front of the building. The patio below on the second floor was a drop of ten or twelve feet, and just off to our left. We also had to get down without attracting the attention of the two rabbits inside. Based on what I had seen, I was counting on the man staying interested long enough for us to get down to the ground.

"Let's hang down off the ledge, work our way a few feet over above the patio, then we should be able to drop down," I whispered. "I'll go first so I can catch you when you drop." She nodded. I crouched down and turned my back to the street, then lowered myself to the point where I was hanging by both hands from the stone ledge. She followed suit and was soon hanging beside me. We started to inch our way along the narrow ledge. At one point, Evelyn lost her grip and I grabbed her arm as she started to slip. She reached back up, got her grip again and we gradually moved to a position just above the second-floor patio. I looked down and saw I was directly over it now. I let go and landed as quietly as I could. We both froze and listened for activity upstairs. The bed springs continued to moan, so Evelyn started up again. When she was just above me, she let go and I caught her before she hit the slate patio.

We both took a deep breath and started down to ground level in the same way we had come up. In a minute, we were back down on the front steps, and then down onto the sidewalk. We both paused and listened before walking away. The bed springs were still taking a beating upstairs. We held hands on the walk back to the hotel, and got the same suspicious eyeball from the front desk clerk as we passed back through the lobby.

When we got back up to the room, I went into the bathroom to wash my face and hands. I wasn't sure what the sleeping arrangements were, so I put on one of the hotel bathrobes. When I came out Evelyn was already lying in bed. The sheets had been pulled back in a way that said she was looking for company. She was wide awake, smiling, and completely naked under the covers. The action back at the Embassy must have gotten to the two of us. I untied my robe and let it drop to the ground, then climbed into bed with her and we did what all newlyweds do on their honeymoon.

Twenty-One: Drive Home

I awoke the next morning, sat up in bed and looked around the hotel room. Evelyn was gone, but her luggage was still standing beside one of the dressers. I got out of bed and checked the bathroom, but it was empty. I took a quick shower and shaved, then came back out with a towel wrapped around my waist. Evelyn had returned to the room and was sitting at the end of the bed holding a small shopping bag in her hand.

"I hope you don't mind, but I went downstairs for coffee and found a very nice men's shop in the lobby. I thought you could use a change of clothes, so I picked something up for you," she offered. "I hope I got your size right?" she asked. I opened the bag and lifted out the shirt and pants, then checked the tags.

"Expensive," I noted. "But the size looks alright." She handed me a coffee.

"Did you find anything last night Nick," she questioned. "We didn't have much time to talk once we got back here," she said blushing. I smiled back and drank some coffee.

"How'd you make out?" I asked. She rolled her eyes at the counter-question. "I didn't know you could read Russian?" I added.

"They teach us all sorts of things at the bureau," she explained. "I didn't find very much, other than some legal records that looked a little interesting," she explained. "Did you find anything?" She questioned again. I walked over to the dresser and pulled the invitation from my pants pocket, then handed it over to her. She read it with interest, then placed it down on the bed beside her.

"Very interesting... That's tomorrow night Nick," she commented. "Does this mean we're going back to Rhode Island?" she asked.

"It does," I answered. "Only by car this time. If we leave right away, we should make it there by nightfall."

"You think Isaac Demidov will be at this dinner party?" She asked.

"He'll be there, and so will we," I replied.

"And that symbol on the invitation… It seems very unusual. Do you know what it is?" she asked.

"It's an outfit I came across a few years back. They call themselves *Oasis*. I'll fill you in on the drive back up," I suggested. I changed into my new clothes and Evelyn packed what we had into her luggage.

"What about tonight? We'll need a place to stay?" she asked. I thought it over for a moment.

"The police are probably camped out at my place, but I've got an idea," I said lifting the receiver on the house phone. I gave the hotel operator the number for the Providence Police. In a minute the line rang, then a switchboard operator answered.

"Providence Police, how may I direct your call," she greeted efficiently.

"Detective Division, Tom Bradley's line," I instructed. She transferred me upstairs.

"Homicide Bureau," a deep voice echoed through the receiver.

"It's me Tom," I greeted. A long heavy exasperated breath exhaled slowly across the line.

"Where in the hell are you Nick?" the voice growled. "They've got half of the state's law enforcement out dragnetting for you," he reported. "Listen pal, just tell me where you are, and I'll send someone by to bring you in safely. Otherwise some trigger-happy officer looking for a promotion might cut you down," he advised.

"I'm in Washington, D.C. Tom," I admitted.

"Tell me you're not making trouble down at that Embassy?" he shouted over the line. "You know I can't help you with the Feds Nick."

"Listen Tom," I interrupted. "Send someone you trust down here to pick me up and I'll come in, but no local police. I've put some of the pieces together and can bring you up to speed as soon as I get back to Rhode Island," I suggested.

"Where are you exactly?" he questioned.

"Just send a couple of good men down here asap. I'll call you back tomorrow and let you know where they can pick me up. When I'm back safely in Providence, I'll fill you in on everything. I know who killed Bridgette Tom," I added before hanging the receiver up. Evelyn smiled at me.

"That's pretty smart Nick. They won't be watching your place if they think you're down here," she commented.

"I have my moments," I agreed. "We'd better get going. He's probably already on the line with the operator to verify that the call came from Washington." I grabbed the luggage and we headed out the door.

When we got downstairs, we checked out at the front desk, then went outside to the valet. It was the same young Mex that had parked the car for me a day earlier.

"Room 814, the Packard," I told him. He nodded and ran off. He returned ten minutes later with the One-Twenty and handed the keys over to me. I pulled a ten-dollar bill from my wallet.

"The police will be by to ask if you saw us leaving the hotel. If they do, you'll tell them we caught a cab… Comprende?" I asked holding the ten spot out in front of him. He nodded his head and took the bill from my hand.

"I understand good mista," he replied. "You and the senora leave hotel in cab. You can count on Pedro," he asserted.

"Good," I replied as we got inside the Packard.

"What about the state police Nick?" Evelyn asked. "The Embassy may have already reported the car as stolen."

"I switched the plates yesterday. We should be alright, especially once we're outside of D.C." I started the engine and we drove off. Evelyn guided me out of the city and soon we were headed north on Route 1.

The ride back to Rhode Island gave Evelyn and I time consider everything that had occurred in the case, starting with Bridgette's murder on Monday morning. It had been a brutal attack, the type done with vengeance in mind. But who would have had that type of gripe with such a sweet kid. No, we both agreed that Bridgette's murder was directed at me. Some case in my past, some client who felt he didn't get his money's worth, some truly evil and ruthless person.

From the start it had been well-planned. Calling the police to my office minutes after the killing, planting the murder weapon in my apartment within hours, sending the police over to search my place, arrest warrants and APB's all within hours of the initial murder. It had been well-planned, the type of coordinated planning that's involves more than one individual, done by a mob of some sort with influence at very high levels.

Then there was Isaac Demidov... He was spotted leaving the scene at the time of the murder and he matched the description of the creep Bridgette had described to me over the telephone. My instincts told me he was the killer. Liam said the man looked pretty well off, with a chauffeured Packard and a golden walking cane. His chauffeur was dead now, I had his Packard, and he had two slugs to the gut coming his way.

His diplomatic position would provide connections in high places, and he was on the Board of Directors at the Turks Head Club. Then there was Otto Demidov, the crazy dentist who tried to put me to sleep permanently. What was his role in all of this? He spoke with Isaac over the telephone and was most likely related in some way, perhaps a brother or cousin. Now the whole thing seemed to be coming to an end with this dinner in Newport tomorrow night. I was sure Demidov would be there, and so would I.

"What do you know about that symbol stamped on the invitation Nick" Evelyn questioned. I pulled the invitation out and glanced down at the ink mark I had made with the stone stamp on Demidov's desk.

"I've seen it once before," I answered. "On a case I worked a few years back. It was supposed to be a quick boat ride over to Amsterdam to pick up a girl named Isabella, then baby sit her on the way back to the states. As it turned out the girl had a secret that some people didn't what to get out, and the trip back got a lot more complicated. The mob that was trying to stop us called themselves *Oasis*, and that symbol was their calling card. I saw them holding court one time and that crest was hanging on the wall behind them. They were well organized, well-connected, and very well-funded. Just the kind of organization that could pull off a job like this," I explained.

"Did you get the girl back safely?" she asked. I nodded.

"Safe and sound," I reported. "Which is more than I can say for some of the goons who tried to stop us." She rolled her eyes at me.

"And you think this Oasis organization may be behind Bridgette's murder?" She questioned.

"Too much coincidence not to be, and I don't believe in coincidence."

"Why would they want to murder Bridgette?" she asked.

"To get to me," I replied. "And they did, but they'll live to regret it."

I didn't mention Alex to Evelyn and wasn't sure why. Alex had helped me bring Isabella back to the states, and now had shown up just a day after Bridgette's murder. She claimed to have been under-cover on assignment all this time. She was connected in some way and I needed to find that answer before this whole thing blew up.

"It was a little after seven when we crossed the Rhode Island state line. It took us another hour to reach the small village of Pawtuxet. We parked the Packard a few blocks away in the lot at Rhodes on the Pawtuxet, then started walking back towards my apartment. As we rounded the corner onto Broad Street, there was an old man seated at the dance hall trolley stop. It was Frank Ingram, so I took the seat beside him on the bench. Evelyn followed suit beside me.

"Hello Frank," I greeted. He reached over and shook my hand.

"Evening Nick," he replied.

"This is a good friend of mine, Evelyn Burroughs." He reached over and shook her hand.

"Nice to meet you Miss," he smiled. She smiled back at him.

"Cops watching my place?" I asked.

"They've been up there for the past couple of days. Must have given up on you because they pulled out this morning," he reported.

"All clear now?" I asked.

"All clear Nick," he answered. I nodded and thanked him. I picked up Evelyn's luggage and we crossed the street, then headed up to my apartment. When we walked in, I pulled down the shades, then lit a small lamp on the kitchen table. She looked around the place.

"I have to say, it's nicer than I expected Nick," she commented. "But where's the bed?" I pointed to the couch.

"It's a pull out," I answered. Just then the telephone started shouting. I let it ring and didn't answer it. It rang a dozen or more times, then stopped. A minute later it started up again. I waited for it to stop so I could take the receiver off the hook. When it did, I lifted the receiver and put it down on the table. A scratchy voice echoed over the line.

"Nick... Is that you?" the voice whispered. I recognized the soft female voice immediately. I lifted the receiver and put it up to my ear.

"Alex?" I questioned. Evelyn's head lifted subconsciously.

"Nick, I can't talk for very long," she said. "You're in danger. You need to meet me tonight in Providence, at midnight under the Shepard's clock."

"What's going on?" I asked.

"I can't talk now… later… tonight," she answered before the line went dead on the other end. I placed the receiver down on the table, leaving it off the hook.

"Who's Alex?" Evelyn questioned.

"Nobody important," I answered. "We better get some sleep. It's going to be a busy day tomorrow." She eyed me suspiciously, then removed some clothes from her luggage and went into the bathroom. I pulled the bed out and lit a smoke. When she came out, she was wearing a sheer negligée that didn't leave much to the imagination. I could see the soft curves of her body in the dim light. She clearly wasn't ready to go to sleep. I looked over at the clock on the wall. It was almost nine. I still had plenty of time. She walked up and kissed me softly, and we picked up where we had left off the night before.

Twenty-Two: Midnight Rendevous

It was almost eleven when Evelyn finally nodded off. I got up gently from the bed, put on some fresh clothes, strapped on the Berretta and headed downstairs.

I was taking a risk going out in the middle of the night to meet with Alex. The police might still be on the lookout for me. There was a chance she was setting me up again to get picked up, but something in her voice seemed genuinely concerned. I crossed Broad Street and walked down to the lot where we had left the Packard. I got in, started the engine and headed downtown.

I found a small alley near the Shepard's department store and parked the car, then sat there in the darkness, waiting for midnight to arrive. When it did, I stepped out and walked down to Westminster Street.

A thick fog from the bay had rolled into the city. Street lights glowed in the heavy mist. I walked under the tall store clock and waited. Ten minutes past with no activity. I pulled a smoke out and set it on fire. When I had finished with the cigarette, I took another look up at the clock. It was twelve-thirty now and still no Alex.

At twelve forty-five, a figure in a trench coat emerged from an alley a few of blocks down and began walking in my direction. I recognized the curves on this particular figure, and knew it was Alex. She walked right up and put her arms around me, then kissed me for what seemed like minutes. When we came up for air, she had an anxious look on her face.

"Nick… You must listen to me," she pleaded. "You're in grave danger. If you turn yourself into the police, it would be the safest place for you right now," she explained.

"What case are you working on," I questioned. "Does it involve Oasis?" She lifted her eyes, then reluctantly nodded.

"Yes… I've spent the last three years infiltrating their organization. I'm finally in a position of confidence Nick. If you keep pressing forward… If you interfere any more than you already have… All my work will have been for nothing."

"Did Isaac Demidov murder Bridgette?" I pressed. Her head bowed in shame, then came back up.

"Yes," she replied hesitantly. "But if you could only lie low for another day or so... Everything is in motion, and Isaac Demidov will soon be in custody Nick."

"I don't want him in custody," I explained. "He's a rabid dog and I'm putting him down Alex. I'm going to give him exactly what he gave Bridgette, and nothing less. You're welcome to whatever's left over when I'm done with him."

"Nick, this is so much bigger than you could possibly realize. It isn't just about a single murder." I interrupted her.

"That's where you're wrong Alex. For me that's exactly what this is about," I explained. "The only thing I need is to gun two slugs into Demidov's gut, then watch him grovel on the ground for his life. He's going down and nobody is going to stop that." She turned away from me in frustration, then spun back to argue her point.

"Oasis has infiltrated governments, disrupted world politics, taken control of labor unions, and undermined world economies. Thousands have suffered and nearly as many have been killed if they dared to get in the way. We need to stop them once and for all, and we finally have an opportunity to capture their leadership in one place over the next day or two." I knew she was referring to the dinner in Newport, but I didn't let on that I knew anything about it.

"Why would Demidov want to kill Bridgette?" I asked. She put her hands in her pockets and rolled her head in frustration.

"It was personal Nick," she replied. "You killed his brother, he kills your secretary. An eye for an eye." I shot a puzzled look back at her.

"Who was his brother?"

"First officer Benson from the SS Santa Rosa, a.k.a. Ivan Demidov," she replied. I thought back a few years to our voyage on the Santa Rosa, and the events leading up to our bringing Isabella back to America. Benson was the ship's first officer and he had been very helpful to me throughout the voyage. But in the end, he revealed himself as an agent of Oasis who tried to stop us, and in the end, it was true that I had killed him.

I looked back at Alex now. She had drawn a forty-five from her trench coat and was pointing it at me. She seemed to be glancing at something over my shoulder. A second voice echoed out somewhere behind me.

"It's time to come in Alex," a female voice stated with authority. I recognized the voice immediately and my stomach did a somersault. I turned and saw Evelyn standing across the street with her Walther PPK drawn and pointed at Alex.

"You tricked me Nick," Alex stated with venom in her eyes. I shook my head.

"I didn't know anything about this Alex," I replied. Evelyn spoke up again.

"Your assignment is over Agent Watson. You've been ordered to stand down and come in with me." Alex looked me square in the eye for a moment, then smiled.

"I believe you Nick," she said. "We'll talk more later." Her gun barked and a bee buzzed close to my waistline. I turned to see where the bullet had landed. Evelyn was lying on the ground now and had dropped the PPK onto the street.

I ran back to her and saw that she had been hit in the lower leg. I picked the gun up and tucked it away in my jacket, then turned to look back at Alex, but she was already gone. I lifted Evelyn up and carried her back to the Packard, laying her down in the back seat. I tore her pants where the bullet had hit to examine the wound.

"She just clipped you," I reported. "You'll be alright." Evelyn looked up at me and smirked. I pulled my handkerchief out and tied it tightly around her calf to stop the bleeding. She grimaced a little when I tightened the knot, but it had to be done. I got in the front seat, started the engine, and got the hell out of there.

Once we were safely out of town, I pulled the car over and let her have it.

"What the hell was that all about!" I shouted back at her. She looked up at me. She was perspiring now, and her skin had gone pale.

"I haven't been completely honest with you Nick," she admitted. "But it appears from that kiss that you haven't been completely forthcoming yourself," she suggested. "Just get me back to your apartment and I'll explain everything," she suggested. I turned forward and shifted the Packard into gear.

Twenty-Three: An Explaination

When I got back, I parked the car behind Lindsey's Market, then carried Evelyn up to my apartment. I laid her down on the bed and went into the kitchen for some supplies. I grabbed the first aid kit from the cupboard, a pair of scissors, a pan, and what was left of my scotch. She was half awake when I got back to her.

"What's all that for?" she asked.

"I need to clean and bandage your wound," I explained. I untied the now blood-soaked handkerchief, and she grimaced a little as I peeled it off. I took the scissors and cut her pants off above the knee.

"How about a shot before we get started?" I asked. Panic flowed down her face.

"Just what are you planning to do Nick?" she asked hesitantly. I lifted her leg and tucked the pan underneath, then moved the lamp up close to examine the wound.

"You're lucky," I said. "The bullet only grazed your calf." She sat up in bed to look at it herself, but her face went pale and she flopped back down.

"I think I'm feeling faint," she said.

"I need to clean out the wound and put a couple of stitches in it. It might hurt a bit," I warned. I lifted the bottle of scotch and offered it to her. She shook her head, so I poured a shot or two directly into the wound. A bloody highball dripped down into the drain pan. She felt it and clenched her jaw. I took a suture out from the first aid kit. She eyed the curved needle and reached her hand out in the direction of the scotch bottle.

"I'll have that drink now Nick," she said. I gave her the bottle and she took a healthy swig from it, then I handed her a bite stick from the first aid case.

"Clamp down on this," I instructed. She bit down, and I did my best needle work, suturing the wound closed. When I was done, I wiped some Mercurochrome on, then wrapped a dressing around her leg.

When I had finished, I looked up and she had either fallen asleep or passed out. Part of me wanted to slap her back into consciousness and question her on what had just happened with Alex, but she wasn't going anywhere so I let her rest. I went back downstairs and moved the car down to the Rhodes parking lot, then headed back.

She was sound asleep when I got upstairs. I took out my smokes and lit one, then drank what was left of the scotch. We were in a risky spot right now. If the cops decided to come by and search my place again, it was all over. I could only hope our diversion had worked, and the police had lost interest in watching my place, at least for tonight. I laid down beside Evelyn and drifted off.

In the morning I went downstairs to Lindsey's Market and picked up some fresh eggs and bacon. I was cooking breakfast on the gas stove when Evelyn finally woke up. She rolled over in bed and looked across the room at me.

"Please tell me that was just a bad dream I had last night?" she asked. I tilted my head to point out the dressing on her leg. She looked down at her bandaged thigh and flopped back down in the bed.

I put some eggs and bacon on a plate for her and carried it over. She sat up in bed and took the food from me, then I went back into the kitchen and made a cup of tea for her. I brought it over and sat down on the edge of the bed.

"So, you're not really an FBI agent?" I questioned. She had a mouthful of food and just shook her head to say that she wasn't. "Then who are you exactly, and how do you know Alexandra Watson?" She finished swallowing her food and took a sip from her tea before answering.

"I'm sorry for not being completely honest with you Nick," she replied.

"That's ok," I answered. "I never actually believed you were an FBI agent, but the badge was useful to us, so I played along."

"What gave me away?" she asked. I laughed.

"FBI agents don't generally carry a small arsenal in their luggage. The standard FBI service revolver is a .38 Smith & Wesson, and you're carrying around a .32 Walther PPK." She took a sip from her tea and then continued.

"It wasn't a complete lie Nick," she explained. "It's true that I'm not an FBI agent, but I am an agent of the British Government, MI6 to be exact."

"That would explain how you know Alex," I said. "Now explain to me what last night was all about?" I added. She handed her empty plate to me and I placed it down on the side table.

"She's not who you think she is Nick," she commented. "You mustn't trust her completely," she advised.

"I don't trust anyone completely," I replied. "But go on." She shot a judgemental glance at me.

"Alexandra Watson was one of our top agents, but we lost contact with her. She was assigned to infiltrate the Oasis organization three years ago. She went under cover and we were receiving regular reports from her during the first year, but then suddenly her communications stopped. We've tried to make contact with her on a number of occasions, but each time she ignored our efforts."

"Where has she been all this time?" I questioned.

"We know that she has spent most of the time in a large estate located in Eastern Europe, Belarus to be exact," she explained. "The Estate spans over a hundred acres and is heavily guarded. At first, we thought Oasis may have caught on to Alex and was holding her against her will. But eventually we spotted the two of them on vacation in Italy one summer, and we realized she was acting on her own."

"The two of them?" I asked. She nodded.

"Yes Nick… Alex and Isaac Demidov. We don't believe Demidov is the leader of Oasis, but he seems to have an important role in the organization. Alex has been living and traveling with him as his… Well as a sort of partner or girlfriend perhaps. Maybe even his wife," she added cautiously. "We're not completely certain as to the nature of their relationship."

"If Demidov isn't their leader, then who is?" I asked.

"We don't know Nick," she explained. "We've come close on several occasions, but he always seems to elude our agents whenever we close in. We've been tipped off once or twice about their secret council meetings, but there are always dozens of Oasis members who attend, and he could be any one of them. The only people who know his actual identity are the members of their high council, which is always held behind locked doors. A few years ago, we were able to apprehend one of the council members, but he took his own life before we were able to question him."

"So, nobody has ever seen the leader?"

"No," she replied. "Just traces, breadcrumbs really. Clues that tell us he does exist, but we've never been able to determine his actual identity. Although MI6 does have a code name for him. They call him the Ghost," she added.

"A Ghost who lurks in the shadows," I commented. "What else?"

"It's been difficult to get to them in Belarus," she explained. "The local authorities are corrupt and on the Oasis payroll. A month ago, we intercepted a communication that told us there was a meeting of top Oasis leaders being held in Rhode Island this week."

"In Newport?" I questioned.

"I didn't know the exact location until you found that invitation Nick," she replied.

"I saw their guest list when I was in Demidov's office. It was a pretty impressive roster," I remarked.

"That's why I came to the states initially, to locate where the meeting was being held, and to find a way inside. We were certain Alex would be there. It was an opportunity to apprehend her and bring her in. If she has turned, she has too much knowledge of the British Government and MI6. My orders are to take her in or ..." She paused to take sip from her tea.

"Go on," I said.

"Or to terminate her if that's not possible," she added.

"Why drag me into this?" I asked.

"We came across the news article earlier this week on Bridgette's death, and we were aware that you and Alex had a past relationship. We didn't know why anyone from Oasis would want to harm Bridgette, but her connection to you was enough to raise eyebrows. I was ordered to find you, in the hope that you might lead me to Alex, or in the event Alex actually came to you."

"Why the charade?" I asked. "Why not play it straight with me from the start?"

"Because I'm a British Agent Nick, and that's what we do," she answered as if that explained everything. "I thought if you believed I was sent by your FBI friend Valentine, you'd be more likely to work with me." I couldn't disagree with her on that point.

"And your story about meeting with Tom and the Providence Police?" I asked.

"That's actually true. I did meet with Detective Bradley, and he told me about the plate you had him run down, along with the information on the Belarus Embassy. That told me you were on the right track, and that you were most likely headed to Washington, D.C. So I bought a ticket on the earliest train south. Our meeting in the New Haven station was simply a bit of good fortune."

"If you're a British agent, where's your accent?" I questioned. She laughed back at me.

"Four years at university, Harvard University in Boston," she replied. "I picked up my American accent during that time," she explained.

"American's don't have accents," I asserted. She smiled.

"Bostonians do," she corrected me.

I thought over everything she had told me, and it added up. She had lied to me, but she was still on the right side of things. She had helped me in New Haven and down in D.C. and I owed her that much. But she couldn't come with me tonight to Newport. My business was with Demidov, and she would have other plans for him.

At lunchtime, I made her a chicken salad sandwich and some more tea. She was starting to look a little better and the color was returning to her face. She was sitting up in bed when I brought the tray over. I placed it down in front of her and she dug in.

"What time should we leave tonight Nick?" She asked eagerly.

"Don't you think you should take a pass on this one and give that leg a rest," I suggested. She shook her head to dismiss the idea.

"I've been tracking down Alexandra Watson for nearly two years, and I'm not going to miss what's probably my best chance to bring her in," she asserted. I nodded in understanding.

"I think if we leave around Five it should give us enough time to catch the six o'clock ferry over to Newport," I replied. "We still have a couple of hours, so rest up while you can," I added. She finished the sandwich and drank what was left of her tea. I took the tray and brought it back to the kitchen, then washed the dishes. An hour later she called me over.

"Nick," she called out in a distressed voice. I went up beside her.

"What's wrong?" I asked.

"I'm not feeling well," she said in a whispered tone now. "I'm feeling quite dizzy and tired."

"Settle down," I comforted her. "It's just the sleeping pill I put in your tea," I admitted. Her eyes rolled up in their sockets as if to scold me, but her voice wasn't cooperating. The medicine was already doing its job. "I'm going after Demidov by myself," I explained. "I'll bring back Alex for you if I can, but I'm taking Demidov down for what he did to Bridgette."

Her hand raised up as if to try and stop me, then fell loosely back to her side as her eyes closed. I checked her pulse and it was fine. The doctor that had given me the sleeping pills said they would put me out for at least four or five hours. By that time, it would be too late for her to stop me. She was in a deep sleep now and I was free to do what had to be done.

Twenty-Four: Chateau Sur Mer:

I changed into my best suit and was heading out the door by four o'clock. I took the Beretta and a full box of ammunition from Evelyn's luggage, along with the knife and invitation I had found in Demidov's office.

When I got down to Rhodes on the Pawtuxet, there was a dance going on and I could hear the band warming up inside. The sun was beginning to set, and kids were already lined up outside to buy their tickets. The Packard was still were I had left it, down close to the river. I got in, started the engine, and drove off. I pulled onto Broad Street, then right onto Post Road and headed south.

I knew I was up against a pretty big outfit this time and considered calling Tom in for assistance. But that would amount to turning myself in, and Demidov might slip away or even get himself arrested. With his connections, he would be free, and on his way back to Belarus within twenty-four hours. Evelyn might have helped me to get inside the party, but in the end, she wouldn't have agreed to what I had in mind for Demidov. What I had in mind was exactly what he had given to Bridgette. I looked down at the pocket-sized Berretta I had borrowed from Evelyn and knew I would be outgunned. I needed some help and a lot more fire power.

I had a quick thought and pulled up to a telephone booth on the roadside. I got out of the car and dropped a nickel into the slot, then dialed a number and the line rang on the other end. A man's voice answered.

"Yeah?"

"Sully," I spoke into the line. "I could use a little help with a party if you're free tonight."

"I got nothing special planned Nick," he answered.

"Can you get yourself down to Newport, on Bellevue Ave just outside of Chateau Sur Mer?" I asked.

"I think I can manage it," he replied. "What time?"

"You'd better leave now," I answered. "Bring a couple of those M1's with plenty of ammo, and maybe that Vickers Mark machine gun you had out back," I suggested.

"Oh… It's that type of party?" he asked.

"It's that type of party," I answered.

"I'm already on my way," he replied before hanging up the receiver. I got back in the Packard and drove off.

It was raining by the time I reached the ferry at Plum Beach. I paid my fare and drove the car on board. It was a short choppy ride over, so I stayed inside the Packard and rolled the window down. I didn't want to take a chance at being spotted by some do-gooder citizen who might alert the police.

The rain was really pouring down by the time we reached Jamestown. I drove across the small island and took the second ferry over to Newport. It was just after seven when I drove off the boat at Newport harbor. Fog and darkness had settled in, and the downpour made visibility that much more difficult.

I drove across town and took an initial pass by Chateau-sur-Mer. It was one of ten head-turning gilded mansions along Bellevue Avenue, all built during the nineteenth century by millionaire titans of industry as summer residences. Chateau-sur-

Mer was a Victorian style estate. Its rough exterior granite softened its facade, which had been modelled after an Italian style villa. I knew the mansion had been owned by Governor Westmore at some point, but that was half a century earlier. I didn't know who owned the property now, but whoever did was clearly connected in some way to Oasis.

As I drove by, I noticed two attendants stationed out in front of a tall wrought iron gate. Cars were pulling in and being directed to park in a lot next to the large stone mansion. The attendants were checking for invitations as the cars entered. I drove past the estate and pulled off to the side of the road, then turned my engine off.

I waited for nearly an hour before a pickup truck rolled up alongside of me. The window came down and I saw Sully seated behind the wheel. A half-smoked cigar hung from his mouth.

"How'd you make out?" I asked.

"We're good to go," He replied through the open window. I nodded back.

"Follow me," I instructed as I pulled the Packard out in front of him. I drove down the street, pulled a U-turn and passed by Chateau-sur-Mer a second time, then took the right just after the mansion. We pulled over half-way down the block under a large oak tree. A short brownstone wall surrounded the perimeter of the large estate. The side road was dark and unlit.

I put my overcoat on and left the Packard running, then walked back to Sully's truck. He rolled the window down. I noticed two M1 Carbines lying on the seat next to him. I glanced in the truck bed and saw an object covered with a canvas tarp. I lifted the canvas and saw the Vickers .30 calibre machine gun mounted on a tripod.

Sully got out of the truck and handed one of the M1's to me.

"It's already loaded, and here's some extra ammo," he said as he handed me a spare magazine. I put the ammo in my jacket pocket. "What's this all about Nick?" he questioned.

"The scumbag that killed Bridgette is in that mansion," I replied. "Along with a Russian-based mob that thinks it can secretly run this country." That was all he needed to hear.

"What's the plan?" he asked. We walked over to the wall and looked across at the expansive estate. It included several cleared acres of well-manicured landscaping, rolling down to the ocean. Aside from the main house, a few oaks dotted the property. A small maintenance building stood in the northwest corner, close to the entrance.

"Take the .30 calibre and station yourself beside that maintenance shed," I suggested. "I need you to cover the entrance gate and make sure nobody leaves here before the police arrive. There are a lot of influential people here tonight, and I want them to get caught with their hand in the cookie jar. If anyone tries to drive out, convince them not to." He nodded and I helped him carry the Machine gun down off the truck bed and over the short wall.

"What's your play Nick?" he questioned.

"I'm driving straight in through the front gate," I said as I pulled the invitation out from my pocket to show him. "When I get inside, I'll find Demidov and that's when the shooting will start. When you hear it, watch for anyone trying to leave. With this wall, they're boxed in and the only way out is through that gate." He nodded.

"What about that rifle?" He questioned. "You'll start a panic walking in the front door with that tucked under your arm." I looked across the lawn at the main building, then handed the M1 back to him.

"I'll have to go in with the just the Beretta," I replied. "Do you think you could make it across and drop the M1 just at the edge of that terrace off the Main house?" I asked. He nodded to say that he could.

"No problem. Give me ten minutes to get over there and drop it off, then a few more to get back on the machine gun," he said. I nodded and shook his hand, then got inside the Packard and drove back onto Bellevue Ave.

As I turned into the driveway at Chateau-sur-Mer, the two attendants at the gate approached my vehicle.

"Your invitation sir," one of them asked. I handed him the invitation and he looked it over quickly. He noticed the special red stamp I had embossed on it while in Demidov's office.

"A private reception for special guests will be held in the Library on the second floor," he said as he handed the invitation back to me. "You can show your invitation to get upstairs sir." I nodded and drove inside.

A couple of young Filipino boys were valeting cars by the front entrance. I parked the Packard myself under a large Oak and turned the engine off, then sat and had a smoke to give Sully enough time to get into position. I checked the Beretta in my shoulder holster, slid the dagger inside my jacket pocket, straightened my tie, and stepped out from the car.

Twenty-Five: Oasis

Guests were still filing in through the front entrance, couples mostly, dressed to the nines. I recognized a few well-known faces from the newspaper. Two U.S. Senators, one governor, several union leaders, a well-known industrialist, a Hollywood actor, two mugs from Federal Hill, and even one famous local athlete. Several white gloved housemen dressed in black tuxedos stood just inside the front entrance offering to take each guest's hat and coat. I handed them my overcoat and walked past them into the hallway.

The place was beyond opulent. There was a double-sided oak stairway running up to the second floor with an elaborate medieval wainscoting on the wall. Both stairways had been roped off. I looked up to the second floor and saw another tuxedoed staff member standing guard at the top of the stairway. This one seemed larger than the others, square jawed, broad shouldered, with a crew cut and face that didn't quite belong.

 I walked back into the main hall and looked up at two railed-in floors above me. A large stained-glass window hung centered in the roof forty feet overhead. The walls were covered with oak and mahogany panelling. French tiled fireplaces with elaborate mantels adorned most of the rooms off the main hall. Most of the guests were filing into a large ballroom with oak parquet flooring. There was a billiards room and a large study with book covered walls. A dining room had been setup as a temporary bar for the evening. I stepped inside and asked the bartender for a drink.

"Scotch," I ordered. The bartender was an aging man in his late sixties. He was tall and reedy, with salt and pepper hair. He wore a black tuxedo that didn't seem to fit him very well. He didn't look as though he wanted to be there. He lifted a bottle of what looked to be very expensive scotch whiskey and poured me a double. I hadn't asked for double, but I must have looked the type to him. I took the glass and knocked it back. He asked if I wanted another, but I waved him off. I needed courage, but not that much courage.

"How do I get out to the patio?" I asked. He pointed to a set of gilded French doors at the back of the room. I dropped a dollar into his silver tip jar and walked outside onto a wide stone patio that spanned half the length of the home. Clouds still covered the night sky, but the rain had tapered off to a light drizzle. There was no one else getting wet outside at the moment. I pulled out a smoke and lit it, then started walking casually along the perimeter of the patio as if I belonged. I noticed the M1 about halfway down, tucked neatly under some short hedgerow. I was still trying to decide how I would get it inside when I noticed some lattice work built into the house, which climbed up to a second story balcony. I picked up the M1, slung it over my shoulder and started up the side of the wall.

There was a short stone pillared rail built along the edge of the balcony. I pulled myself up and over. The room leading out to the small terrace was darkened. Another set of large French doors led inside. I tried at the brass knob and it turned, so I opened the door and went quietly inside.

It took a moment for my eyes to adjust to the darkness, but things gradually came back into focus. It was a large bedroom, with a king-sized canopied bed on one side, and a set of mahogany dressers on the opposite wall. A tall gilded mirror stood between the two dressers, rising from floor to the ceiling. The room didn't look as though it had been occupied any time recently. Most likely intended for the occasional guest visiting on vacation over the summer.

I slung the M1 Carbine down from my shoulder and pulled the action back to chamber the first .30 calibre brass round inside, then walked to the door and cracked it open. The large doorman was still stationed at the top of the stairway with his back to me. Just then, a guest appeared at the top of the stairs and the large sentry took his invitation to examine it. It was apparently genuine, and the guard removed the rope at the top the stairs to let the man pass by. The guest walked a few doors down the hallway and entered the last door on the right.

I stepped quietly out into the hallway and approached the large sentry from behind. A live brass band was playing music downstairs now, which covered the sound of my footsteps on the parquet floor. As I approached, I lifted the rifle and hammered the stock down heavy on the back of his head. He felt it and dropped to one knee for a moment, then regained his footing and turned to face me. He was holding a six-inch knife in his right hand now and smiling back at me. I knew a shot from the M1 would take care of him but would only draw attention to me and give time for Demidov to escape.

He lunged at me with his knife as I side-stepped him, blocking his wrist with the rifle, then driving the butt of the gun square into his throat. The knife dropped to the ground. The band music continued to play downstairs as he reeled back grasping at his throat. He was gasping for breath now, but he was tough and wasn't going down easily. I unlatched the rope on the stairway and waited for his next attack. It came a moment later as he charged at me with both hands outstretched. I parried his attack again and got behind him this time. As I did, I swung the rope around his thick neck and tightened it as he passed by. I clamped down on the rope and held it as tight as I could. He fought and tried to loosen my grip, but it was wasted effort. His knees buckled, and his lifeless body fell limp to the ground. I stood still for a second to see if anyone from the room at the end of the hallway came out. No one did.

I dragged him into the bedroom and shut the door, then returned the rope to the top of the stairs to discourage anyone else from coming up. I picked the M1 up off the ground and walked towards the end of the hallway. As I approached the last door, I heard men's voices talking inside. I put my ear up to the heavy door but couldn't make much out through the thick mahogany. I tried the doorknob, but it was locked, then thought about knocking but there was a judas window in the door and someone would have to identify me before letting me inside.

I doubled back to the bedroom and stepped over the lifeless sentry, then back outside onto the wet balcony. I looked across at a second balcony about six feet over from the one I was standing on. Thunder crackled somewhere in the darkened sky.

It was a healthy jump, but one I thought I could make. I slung the M1 over my shoulder and climbed up onto the short stone wall, then took a few steps backwards. I got a running start and jumped across to the second balcony. I landed hard on the stone railing, got my grip and climbed over the top. When I stood up, I looked out across the expansive lawn below, then over to the small work shed in the corner of the property. Lightning flashed, and I could see the barrel of the Vickers .30 Calibre protruding out from the edge of the shed, along with the intermittent burn of a cigar hanging from Sully's mouth.

There were three sets of French doors winding around the side of the building. The first two sets were darkened inside, but light was coming from the last pair and one of the two doors was cracked open. I drew the M1 out in front of me and walked quietly up to the doorway. The wind was gusting now, and the rain began beating down hard again on the stone balcony. As I approached, I heard men's voices talking inside. One man's voice in particular seemed to dominate the conversation. He spoke with a thick eastern European accent and seemed to be chastising someone else inside the room.

"Comrade… You have not explained to this council's satisfaction the deficit in your division's performance during this past quarter," he shouted sternly. I peered through the crack in the door and saw the man who was doing the shouting. He was seated at the head of the large walnut table. I could see several other men seated near him. He had black eyes with bushy eyebrows, greasy black hair, a dark complexion, and an extravagant handlebar moustache waxed up on either side. I remembered Bridgette's words to me over the telephone. "He's a queer bird Nick," she had described. I remembered the photo of Isaac Demidov in the Board room at the Turk's Head Club. It was Demidov alright. I levelled the M1 in his direction. It was all I could do to stop myself from pulling the trigger right there and then, but I wanted him to know who it was coming from. The man he was speaking to eventually responded.

"I am sorry to report that we were unable to maintain our profit margins this past quarter," he explained. "But the current authorities in our precinct have demanded more in payment over the past few months. We have been forced to double our customary payoffs," he explained. Demidov became furious, standing up and pounding his two fists on the table.

"Then eliminate the current authorities and replace them with more reasonable ones," he demanded. "This organization must never give in to this type of demand, which only displays weakness. We must always be ruthless and feared by our adversaries."

"It will be done number two," the second man assured him. His response seemed to appease Demidov who eased back down into his chair. Just then, a doorway opened and everyone at the table stood up.

"Hail to our Leader!" the sleaze-ball shouted before quickly shifting to the next seat at the table. The group sat down slowly, then I heard a set of footsteps approaching on the parquet floor. Within a moment the leader came into view and took her seat at the head of the table. It was Alex.

"Why is this room unguarded?" she demanded. The group looked around at each other dumbfounded. I decided it was time to introduce myself to Oasis. I kicked the door in and walked inside with the M1 levelled directly at Demidov.

"He wasn't feeling very well," I explained. "So I told him to take the rest of the night off." A few of the more dubious looking men at the table began to reach under their jackets for their iron.

"Don't even think about it!" I shouted pointing the M1 at Alex's head. "Guns on the table gentleman and do it slowly!" I instructed. They all looked immediately at Alex for direction. She nodded for them to do as I had said. Six of the twelve guests reached slowly under their jackets and placed their weapons down on the table. There were two women seated at the end of table, so I instructed one of the them to collect the guns and bring them over to me. She did as I asked and then took her seat again.

"What's the meaning of this intrusion?" Demidov shouted as he stood up. "This is a private affair and we can have the police here within minutes." I looked over at Alex, but she said nothing.

"Sit your ass down!" I shouted levelling the gun back at him. "We'll have some law here tonight, but not just yet Demidov," I explained. "First we're going to get to know one another a little better." His face painted red and his black eyes shot venom at me. Alex sat calmly at the head of the table with a deadpan face.

"Since you already seem to know who we are, it seems only reasonable that you tell us who you are?" Demidov questioned.

"His name is Nick Chambers," Alex spoke up. The group all turned and looked at me as if the name meant something to them. Demidov squirmed in his seat, wanting to do something but not being able to. I walked over to him.

"Let's talk about another name Isaac. One that belonged to an innocent young girl. Her name was Bridgette. This girl had her throat slit by a little coward who didn't have the guts to face me himself." He looked up and smiled at me. I slammed the rifle stock across his sick face and he went to the ground. "Stand up and take your beating like a man you piece of garbage!"

"Nick!" Alex interrupted. I looked over at her.

"Go out and call the police," I instructed. She paused for a second, then nodded and left the room. The rest of the group look puzzled by her actions, but quickly placed their focus back on Demidov who was climbing back to his feet. A stream of blood was trickling down the side of his greasy head now. I slammed the gun stock back across his face a second time and his head bounced off the table. I bent over and whispered into his ear.

"There won't be any police for you Isaac," I explained. I went back to the head of the table and addressed the people seated around it.

"I recognize most of your ugly mugs from the papers, but just to make sure I get the names right, why don't you go ahead and write them down for me," I instructed, tossing a small pad and pencil across the table. It landed in front of one of the women, who reached out to write her name down. Demidov spoke up.

"Don't give him anything," he told the others. "He'll be dead soon and he won't have any use for such a list."

"Someone in this room is going to be dead soon, but it ain't going to be me pal. I'm not a defenseless little girl. But if you think you're up to it, I'll play along," I added pulling the dagger from my jacket. I tossed it down on the table directly in front of him. His eyes bugged at the stainless-steel blade, only a foot away from his grasp. He wanted to grab it and drive the blade through my neck, just as he had with Bridgette. He stared at the weapon intently for almost a minute. The room was silent as he debated whether to try for it, but he eventually eased back down into his chair. I laughed at him just as Alex came back into the room.

"Ok Isaac, let's say we give you a fair chance." Alex walked up beside me and touched my arm. I handed her the M1 and turned to Demidov.

"Here's your opportunity scumbag… I'm completely unarmed," I nudged. "Come on tough guy!" I shouted. "Big man who likes to cut little girls. Let's see if you can do the same to me?" I prodded. The other members at the table turned their attention to him. His eyes glossed over, and he smiled back at me, then he lifted the knife from the table as he stood up to face me.

"I'll gut you like I did your little wench," he threatened. I pulled the Beretta from my shoulder holster and pointed it at him.

"That's all I wanted to hear," I replied. I could see the group shift their attention to Alex who was standing behind me now.

"Surprised about my friend," I commented. "Well, sometimes people aren't who you think they are." Just then I felt the cold barrel of the M1 kiss the back of my neck.

"I'm sorry Nick. Put the gun down," Alex ordered. "If you don't, I'll be forced to pull the trigger," she added for clarity. I sighed and placed the Beretta down on the table. As I did, one of the goons seated to the left grabbed the weapon and pointed it directly at me.

"That's ok," I said. "I had to know one way or the other… and now I know," I added looking back at her.

Demidov laughed and seemed to relax a bit now. He spun the dagger in his hand as if he knew how to use it.

"Let me finish him?" the goon holding my Berretta asked.

"No guns," Alex commanded. "Remember the crowd downstairs," she reminded everyone. Demidov walked closer to me and smiled.

"Fortunately, guns will not be necessary Leader. This blade will do the job, and it will do it quietly," he suggested to Alex. "This one's mine," he asserted looking directly at me now. "You killed my brother three years ago Mr. Chambers. Do you even remember him?" he questioned.

"I remember him now," I answered. "When I walked in here tonight I smelled the same rotten stench on you, and it reminded me of him." He struck the knife quickly down across my cheek. The blade cut in just below my eye. I felt blood running down my face now. He was quick, and I could see how Bridgette would never have stood a chance against him.

"Now I kill you, just as I killed your little whore," he said spinning the knife in the palm of his hand. Suddenly, a shot rang out in the room. The man who was holding the Beretta on me flopped down onto the table. Blood leaked out from his skull. His eyes were still wide open, but he was dead. I looked up at the door where Sully stood holding his own M1 on the group.

"Anybody moves, they die," he stated in a simple but convincing manner.

Demidov didn't pay attention to him and lunged at me with his blade. I side-stepped, grabbed his wrist with my left hand and drove my right fist deep into the side of his throat. His eyes rolled back inside his of skull. His grip on the knife unconsciously loosened, and the blade dropped onto the table. While still holding his arm down, I snatched the knife up quickly with my right hand and thrust it into his carotid. He stood still for a moment, before falling casually back down into his chair. The dagger was still protruding from his neck. Blood gushed out, but he didn't seem to mind.

Sully fired a second warning shot and covered the rest of the mob at the table with his M1. They all heard it and sat back down in their seats. I picked up the Berretta and walked over to Demidov. His eyes were still working, staring around the room and wondering what had just happened. Blood continued to spray from the side of his neck.

"That was from Bridgette," I whispered into his ear. "But this is from me," I added as I squeezed on the trigger twice, sending two lead slugs into his gut. His eyes rolled shut one last time. He was dead.

Twenty-Six: Alex

Sully turned around and bolted the heavy door shut. He puffed on the cigar still hanging from his face and the tip came to life.

"When you didn't come down, I figured you could use a hand," he said. "I called your detective pal just before I came inside. The police should already be on their way," he reported. I nodded and turned to look back at Alex. The French doors to the balcony were open and she had vanished.

The band had stopped playing, and you could hear a commotion taking place downstairs. Engines were turning over in the parking lot and tires were screeching out on Bellevue Avenue.

"Sounds like the mob downstairs is leaving in a hurry," Sully commented.

"That's ok pal," I replied. "We've got the most important guests right in this room. Hold them here until the police arrive. I'm going after their leader," I said. He nodded and pulled a lighter from his pocket, then resuscitated the half dead cigar he had clenched between his teeth.

"No worries bud. Nobody here is leaving any time soon," he commented as he levelled the M1 at the group. I nodded and tucked the Beretta back in my shoulder holster, then ran outside.

The rain was pouring down hard now, and a heavy wind was gusting across the large oceanfront property. I looked across the length of the balcony, but Alex was already gone. I peered out over the railing and scanned the expansive lawn sloping down to the rocky ocean front. A small dark figure was running across the property in the direction of the water. I climbed over the stone railing and lowered myself down until I was hanging five or six feet from the patio below, then let go and dropped down onto the flagstones.

When I stood up, I peered out across the rear of the property. She was just a small dot on the landscape now. I bolted out onto the lawn and sprinted through the downpour after her. I felt as though I was gaining on her when she suddenly disappeared from my view. She had reached the edge and was heading over the side now. I ran for another minute or so until I reached the same cliff. It was a steep hundred-foot drop to a bottom of jagged rock and brush. There was a stairway built into the side of the cliff that zig-zagged its way down to the bottom. She was already halfway down by the time I stepped onto the staircase.

I started down the stairs as quickly as I could, stumbling a few times on the slippery steps. The rain was driving hard and making it difficult to see the small beach at the bottom. When I hit the sand, she was running up onto a small dock about fifty yards away. There was a motorboat tied to the dock, and she was headed for it. I sprinted across the beach and up onto the small pier.

She was already in the boat when I got there. It was a two-seater barrel-back Chris Craft with an American flag mounted on the stern. The engine was already running, and Alex was seated behind the wheel on the right-hand side. By the time I reached the boat I was completely winded. She had a revolver drawn and was pointing it directly at my chest.

"If you wouldn't mind untying that bow line Nick," she asked casually.

"Sure, just give me a second to catch my breath," I replied. She smiled back at me.

"You spoiled my party Nick," she commented. "Now I have to leave early."

"I'm sorry about that, but imagine my surprise when I found out you were leading that pack of misfits," I answered. "Just who's side are you on anyway?" I asked.

"I'm on my side Nick," she answered. "You couldn't understand what I've been through. All those years, putting my life on the line for Queen and country, and where did it get me?"

"So you decided to turncoat and join Oasis, then worked your way up to becoming their supreme leader?" I questioned.

"Why not," she shot back. "Isaac was an imbecile, and certainly not up to the role. When you killed his brother, it created a vacancy and I decided to step up."

"Since your bringing up Isaac, just what was your relationship with that little weasel?" I asked. She smiled and pointed to the bow.

"Are you jealous Nick? That's good to know. Now please untie that line," she said levelling the revolver at me. I bent down and untied the line from the cleat, but held the rope in my hand.

"Well?" I pressed.

"I agreed to marry him initially to gain his confidence, and to gain complete access to Oasis," she explained. "But there was never anything real between the two of us Nick," she added.

"Then why let it go on for so long?" I asked.

"I was building credibility within the organization. But once I saw the true wealth and scope of Oasis, the power and control it had over politicians, industry and labor unions, and in many instances entire governments..." she paused. "Even your great country is controlled to some extent by members of our organization. I simply couldn't walk away from that, not after working so hard to gain the position I had."

"That's a touching story," I replied. "It should play well with the feds when they get here." She smiled at me through the rain.

"I don't plan on being here when they arrive," she answered. "If only the circumstances were different Nick. Who knows how things might have turned out between us? We might have been married at some point, maybe even honeymooned at Niagara Falls."

"We still could," I lied.

"I don't think the authorities would allow it Nick," she replied. "But it's sweet of you to offer just the same. Now throw that rope onto the bow and turn around," she ordered ominously. I tossed the rope on the boat and stood facing her. "Turn around Nick," she ordered.

"No," I answered calmly. "If you're going to shoot me, you'll have to look me straight in the eyes when you do it." She spun the boat around and pointed the bow out to sea, keeping the barrel of her revolver levelled in my direction. She gave the engine a little gas and the boat started out slowly. She kept her gun trained on me.

"Remember what I told you Nick," she shouted through the rain. "Maybe there is still hope for us after all." She put the gun down on the seat beside her and gunned the throttle. All six cylinders in the rear engine roared and the small craft began cutting through the rough surf on its way out to sea. I pulled the Berretta from my shoulder holster and took aim at the engine in the boat's stern. My finger hugged the trigger for a moment, trying to decide if it should pull back. The boat grew smaller and smaller on its way out, eventually disappearing completely into the storm. I lowered the gun and tucked it away in its holster. I thought about her last words to me, *remember what I said to you*, she had remarked. "Maybe… Just maybe," I thought to myself.

Twenty-Seven: The Law Steps In

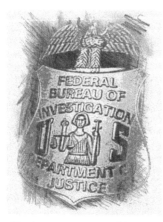

By the time I had climbed back up, I could see the red lights on the squad cars parked in front of Chateau-sur-mer. I walked back across the expansive lawn to the terrace off the dining room and entered through the tall French doors. The bartender had left his post and the room was empty now. I walked up to the bar and poured myself a tall highball, then drank it down as I tried to catch my breath. A young officer opened the door and stepped into the room.

"The party's over mister," he informed me. "All guests are being questioned in the ballroom."

"I'm Nick Chambers," I said. He drew his revolver out and aimed it at me. Too many people were pointing guns at me today. He seemed a little shaky, so I tried to calm him down.

"No guns are necessary officer," I assured him. "I'm turning myself in." I reached both hands out in front of me to be handcuffed. He kept the revolver trained on me and took his cuffs out, then came over and slapped them tightly down on my wrists.

"I think your boss will want to see me upstairs," I suggested. He smiled back at me.

"Yeah, and I'm the guy who brought you in," he complimented himself.

"Congratulations," I offered. He put his gun away and shoved me back out into the main hallway. As we passed the ballroom, I looked inside and saw almost a hundred irritated people standing around, waiting to be questioned. Two officers stood guard at the base of the stairs as we approached.

"I got that Chambers suspect here," he reported proudly. "He's a wanted man, so I'll take him upstairs to the brass." The two officers eyed me up and down, then unlatched the rope at the base of the stairway to let us pass. We walked upstairs and he took me back into the study.

The Oasis council members were still seated where they had been. Demidov was slumped over dead in his seat, while two officers removed the second dead man from the table. They picked him up and carried him back out into the hallway. Sully sat at the head of the table, one arm handcuffed to a chair. A large officer holding his M1 stood guard just behind him. Someone who looked like the local sheriff stood over Demidov examining his injuries.

"Excuse me Sir," the young officer spoke up. "I captured Chambers downstairs and thought you would want to see him." The sheriff turned and shot a surprised look at the officer, then gave me the once over. He was an old-timer who had more than likely worked on the Newport Police force all his life. He was in his seventies with thinning grey hair that had lost some ground on top. He wore a Stetson on his head and his revolver hung cowboy style on his hip. Some of these local town cops still liked playing wild west, but judging by his age he may have had some real-life experience.

"Sit him down next to his friend," he ordered. The officer led me to the end of the table and shoved me down into the blood-stained seat just vacated by the dead man they had carried off. There was still blood pooled on the table along with fragments of brain matter that had come from Sully's rifle shot.

"A lot of folks out looking for you Mr. Chambers," the sheriff commented. "Could I ask what brings you down to our neck of the woods."

"I came here to kill him," I said nodding across the table at what was left of Demidov.

"That so?" he commented to himself. "Pretty thorough work by the look of things."

"I suppose so," I answered. "He was second man in charge of an international crime ring that call themselves Oasis. I'm a private detective out of Providence. His name was Isaac Demidov and he murdered my secretary five days ago. These people are all members of Oasis and they were having some type of twisted council meeting when I arrived here tonight. This man is my associate and I instructed him to hold these people here until the police arrived. You'll want to call the FBI in on this Sheriff," I added.

"Will I now?" the sheriff replied. He looked over at the large officer standing guard behind Sully. "What do you think Jackson? Do we need to bring the FBI in on this one, or do you think our small-town minds can handle it?" Officer Jackson laughed and nodded back at him. The sheriff walked back over to Demidov to have another look.

"Pretty messy situation we have on our hands here," he commented. "But I'll tell you what I think mister... I'm sick and tired of city folk like yourself coming down to our little town and leaving this type of garbage behind for the rest of us to clean up. You already confessed to one of these murders, so as far as I'm concerned, this case is already half solved. How about making things easy and confessing to the second killing?"

"Alright Sheriff, why not," I replied. He smiled back at me.

"See Jackson, he's cooperating."

"I'm a cooperator," I reassured him.

"Same here," Sully piped in.

"Glad to hear it fellas," he said. "Well that's two bodies and two confessions. I'd say that's a pretty decent night's work." Just then two large men in hats and trench coats burst into the room. The sheriff looked across the long table at them. "You men aren't allowed up here," he ordered. They ignored him and began walking towards the head of the table.

The Sheriff nodded to the large officer, who stepped in the path of one of the two men. The man was Detective Tom Bradley. Tom had a couple of inches on the officer and was holding both of his hands in his pockets. The detective walking just behind Tom held a sawed-off shotgun in his right hand. As the young officer put his arm out, Tom's right hand withdrew from his pocket holding a blackjack. The ball of lead came cracking down hard against the officer's skull. The man was big, but he fell hard and didn't get up. Tom was not a cooperator.

"Who the hell are you fellas?" the sheriff shouted, still holding a shaky hand over his six-shooter. Tom showed him his buzzer and the second man pulled out a golden version of his own.

"Detective Bradley, Providence Police," Tom explained. "This is federal agent Russell from the FBI. We're in charge here now sheriff." The old man looked at the two imposing detectives, then lifted his hand off the gun on his hip, and reluctantly gave in.

"City folk," he commented in disgust, then walked out from the room. Tom looked at me and then at Sully.

"I should have known that this one was helping you Nick." Sully looked up at Tom but said nothing. "Who's the stiff?" Tom asked.

"His name was Isaac Demidov," I answered. I saw Tom's head shake back and forth in frustration.

"The diplomat?" He questioned. I nodded my head to say that it was. "And who are all of these people?"

"They're all members of Oasis Tom, important members. Some sort of secret council that ran the organization," I explained. "Demidov was second in command and he admitted tonight to killing Bridgette."

"Can anyone else testify to that?" Tom asked.

"All of these upstanding citizens were here in the room when he did," I reported. "It shouldn't take much to beat the truth out of them." Tom looked the group over and smiled. Three more Providence officers entered the room. Tom motioned to them.

"Take this bunch downstairs and arrest the lot of them. We'll question them all back at the station. The officers nodded and started herding the group out the door. One man sat unmoved in his seat and shot an empty stare across the table.

"Let's go pal," one of the officers nudged at him. Suddenly, something cracked inside the man's mouth and a white foam bubbled out over his lips. The officer grabbed a hold of him, but the man's head was already slumped forward. Tom ran over and lifted his head off the table.

"Cyanide," Tom commented. "Well… I suppose that's one less trial for the taxpayers to pay for. Take him and the other stiff outside down to the coroner's wagon. Be sure to search the others," he ordered to the officers. In a few minutes the room had been cleared aside from myself, Tom, Agent Russell, and Sully. Tom took the seat where Demidov had been and motioned for agent Russell to do the same.

"Ok Nick, start from the beginning and don't even think about leaving something out."

"I could use a smoke?" I said.

"Same here," Sully added. Tom pulled a pack from his wallet and threw it on the table along with his lighter. I lifted the pack with my cuffed hands and pulled two cigarettes out. I handed one to Sully and stuck one in my mouth, then used the lighter to set them both on fire.

"It's a big operation Tom," I explained. "They call themselves Oasis. I ran into this mob over in Europe a few years ago. I was on a job for your boss Russell, only he was just Agent Valentine at the time. Anyway, back then I had a chance to listen in on one of their secret council meetings, and believe me when I tell you this mob is into everything. Rigged elections, extortion, union breaking, political payoffs, right down to paid assassinations. They've infiltrated most governments and are better funded then most countries." Tom nodded.

"Agent Russell already filled me in on some of the background Nick," Tom reported. "Go on with your story."

"It was on that same job three years ago when I ran into Demidov's brother. I thought he was playing for the right team at first, but eventually I realized he was part of this Oasis outfit. He came at me on the trip back and… Well, let's just say I was the one who walked away. Anyway, Demidov was looking for payback for his brother's death, so he murdered Bridgette earlier this week." I stopped for a minute and took a long drag on my smoke, then went on.

"After Bridgette was killed, I tracked Demidov down to the Turks Head Club. I was able to get a look at a picture of him hanging on the wall there. He fit the description of the man Bridgette had given me over the telephone on the morning she was killed."

"From there, I headed south down to D.C. I had the address you had given me on the license plate seen leaving my building on Monday morning, the one belonging to the Belarus Embassy. I got some help from a British agent by the name of Evelyn Burroughs of MI6. She was in the states trying to track down Alexandra Watson. Alex was a British Agent who had gone under cover to infiltrate Oasis.

That was over three years ago, and MI6 hasn't been able to make contact with her since."

"I can confirm that much of the story," Agent Russell interjected.

"I met Agent Burroughs myself on Tuesday," Tom admitted.

"Alex reached out to me earlier this week and told me my life was in danger. She advised that I go into hiding for a few days until things blew over," I explained.

"Did you?" Tom asked.

"Not exactly… I headed to D.C. with Agent Burroughs and we were able to search the Belarus Embassy." I noticed Tom's eyes roll as he rubbed the back of his neck. I took in some smoke and went on with my story.

"While we were inside, we found Demidov's office and came across some spare invitations to the party tonight at Chateau-sur-mer. Alex had mentioned that something big was going down with Oasis, and whatever it was, it was happening this week. I knew Demidov would be here and I guessed that Alex would be too." Agent Russell interrupted.

"Did you have anything to do with Demidov's chauffeur being found dead at the base of the Washington Monument yesterday?" he asked. "Or a man who was found stabbed to death on the railroad tracks in New Jersey?"

"No to both questions," I answered.

"Better give it to us straight Nick!" Tom advised. "The bodies have been piling up all week and you seem to be the only common denominator. We can't help you if we don't have the whole picture. Otherwise something is bound to come back and bite you in the ass."

"Ok, then yes to both questions." I admitted. "Both of those thugs worked for Oasis, both came gunning for me, and both were cases of self-defense." Agent Russell shot a doubtful look across the table at Tom.

"Where is agent Burroughs now?" Tom asked.

"She's at my place resting. Last night Evelyn tried to bring Alexandra Watson in, but Alex shot her in the leg and escaped."

"Keep talking Nick," Tom instructed.

"Well, I knew I was up against a pretty big outfit, so on my way down here, I called in Sully for backup. When I got here tonight, they were having one of their secret council meetings up in this room. Demidov seemed to be leading the meeting, until their real leader walked in."

"Who was that?" Agent Russell asked with a sudden heightened interest.

"Alexandra Watson," I replied. "I thought she might just be playing the part at first, but now I'm not so sure."

"The second British agent?" Tom asked.

"That's right," I replied pumping more smoke down into my lungs. "Agent Burroughs tried to warn me that Alex had turned, but I didn't want to believe her. I couldn't believe it without seeing Alex again for myself. But she looked me in the eye tonight and I think I believe it now. Anyway, Alex escaped through the back of the property and climbed down the side of the cliff. She had a small motorboat tied up down on the beach."

"You let her get away?" Agent Russell asked.

"I guess I did," I admitted. You could see the disappointment roll down his long face.

"What else?" Tom pressed.

"That's all of it Tom, or most of it at least, other than a guest list I picked up from Demidov's office. The list is back at my place, but the council members were all seated at this table tonight." I explained.

"They're on their way into the station now, and everyone downstairs is being questioned before they're allowed to leave," Tom explained.

"No other bodies yet to be discovered?" Tom questioned. I thought about the dentist and hedged, then just shrugged my shoulders.

"Alright Nick," Tom said as he stood up. "You're under arrest."

Greetings From NIAGARA FALLS

Twenty-Eight: Niagara Falls

Sully and I walked out of prison three months later. They had held us over for trial, and we both gave state's evidence against the members of Oasis who had been rounded up that night at Chateau-sur-mer. We were free men again, but I wasn't able to get my license reinstated. I had killed four men, and that wasn't sitting well with the District Attorney, but the evidence I had supplied was enough to let me breathe fresh air again. Demidov was dead, and hopefully had no other living siblings for me to worry about. All of the still living Oasis members seated at the table that night had been arrested and tried in federal court. Most had been convicted and were looking to spend the rest of their lives in federal prison.

One guest at the table that night was acquitted by his jury. He was a dashing Hollywood movie star who had peaked in the thirties. He seemed to have won over the female members of his jury with his testimony. The star-struck jury was dead-locked, and he walked away a free man, but his acting career was long over.

Oasis had lost its second in command, along with most of their secret council members by the time the last trial had concluded. The only member to escape scot-free had been Alex. I shook Sully's hand and thanked him for his help.

"Anytime Buddy," he replied.

"What now?" I asked.

"I'll go back to my shop and do what I do," he replied. "Assuming those young punks haven't robbed my blind by now," he said smiling. He took a half-smoked cigar from his jacket and resurrected it, then hailed a cab and headed back to Olneyville.

I walked a few blocks across town, then rode the elevator back up to my office. Dusty police tape was still hanging loosely across the doorway to my office. I tore it down and went inside. A stack of mail from the past several months was piled up on the floor where the mailman had deposited my letters through the door slot. I looked over at Bridgette's vacant desk and suddenly felt empty inside. There was still a large dried blood stain on the oak floor. I carried the mail into my office and dropped it down on the desk, then went back out to the reception area and washed the floor down.

When I had finished, I went back into my office and poured myself a highball, then sat down and began opening the mail. There was a handful of overdue utility bills, a few letters from lawyers who had seen my name in the paper and wanted to offer their services to me, a letter from the landlord threating eviction, half a dozen requests from local reporters to interview me, and one notice to renew my ad in the yellow pages.

I was getting to the bottom of the stack when I cut open an envelope and five crisp hundred dollar bills spilled out onto my desk. There was no note with the cash, just a postcard with nothing written on it. The postcard was from Niagara Falls. I examined the outside of the envelope and saw the postmark was from Sioux Falls, South Dakota. I thought about Alex's last words to me, and then about the reach of Oasis.

A week later I had checked into the Hotel Converse on First Street in Niagara Falls, N.Y. It was a longshot finding Alex, but something inside me told me I had to finish things with her. I spent the first week roaming Queen Victoria Park, looking for Alex and getting some decent exercise in the process. By week two I was taking daily rides on the Maid of the Mist and had gotten to know the captain pretty well. By the end of the second week, I had begun to get discouraged. I gave him my card and my address at the Converse. He agreed to call me if he saw anyone matching Alex's description. I spent that weekend at Prospect Park on the American side, but still came up empty.

On Monday, I decided to take a tour of the tunnels beneath the falls. It was one of the only places I hadn't visited yet. I bought my ticket and joined the tour group. We put on the raincoats and boots they provided, then headed downstairs in an elevator.

When I stepped out of the elevator, I immediately felt a cold wind gusting in from the falls outside. Our guide led us through the damp tunnel and out onto a red wooden stairway build into the side of the falls. The stairs led down along the rocks to an observation deck that was very close to the falling water. Our guide led us up to the platform, where mist from the falling water soaked our entire group.

As we stood there getting drenched, I noticed a second tour group heading back up the stairway. The figure of a woman in the back of the crowd looked familiar to me. The tour group climbed the stairs and started back inside the tunnel. When the woman reached the top of the stairway she turned back and looked out across the falls. She stood there for almost a minute, as if to give me a chance to really look her over. It was Alex alright. She turned suddenly and went inside.

I sprinted away from my tour group and ran back up the winding staircase. I was completely winded when I reached the top and headed directly back inside the tunnel entrance. A third group of tourists was exiting as I stepped inside and pulled down the hood on my raincoat. I looked at every face that passed me on the way out, but I didn't see Alex. I ran down the tunnel back to where the elevators were, just in time to see the door closing on the last car going up. I pressed the up button and waited impatiently.

As I stood there, I heard something crack in the tunnel off to my left, then what sounded like footsteps on the cement floor. I started down the damp passageway and eventually reached a shorter connecting tunnel that led directly out under the falls. Millions of gallons of water were falling hard at the tunnel's end. There was a short gate maybe six feet from the edge, warning tourists not to pass beyond that point. On the opposite side of the gate stood Alex. Her face and hair were soaked, and she wore a long white trench coat that hugged her hips.

She held her hands in her pockets and looked calmly back at me.

"I was beginning to wonder if you ever received my postcard Nick," she greeted.

"It took some time to work things out with the Feds," I replied. "But we did ok in the end."

"I'm glad to hear it," she answered.

"I think you're standing on the wrong side of that railing," I noted. She looked back over her shoulder at the falling water and then back at me.

"Where do you stand Nick?" she questioned.

"What do you mean?"

"Did you come here by yourself?" She asked.

"You think I dragged the cops all the way up here?" I smiled. She walked up to the railing and stood by it. I went up close to her, then reached across and kissed her. It was a long kiss, the kind you hope will never end. When it did, she looked at me with those soft chestnut eyes.

"I have enough money for us to live comfortably for the rest of our lives Nick," she offered. "We can travel the world and go anywhere that you like."

"Except home," I answered. "We would never be able to get back into the states, or even into Great Britain for that matter. We would always have a price on our heads, running from the law and looking over our shoulder."

"It wouldn't be that way Nick. I have connections and enough money to take care of the two of us for the rest of our lives. We can finally be together and who knows, maybe even take that honeymoon?" I reached inside my pocket and pulled out the small Berretta I had grown an affection for.

"I'm taking you in Alex," I said coolly. Her face went stiff and her soft eyes suddenly hardened.

I'm not going back Nick," she said turning her back to me. "You'll have to shoot me."

"If that's how it needs to be," I replied stoically. She spun back around with tears in her eyes now, reaching her arms behind my neck and kissing me again. It was a deep passionate kiss, the type of kiss that would melt away most men's worries. When she was done, she took a step back and looked deep into my eyes, then down at the gun in my hand as if to ask me to put it away. I kept it leveled at her.

"You'd throw away everything between us just to bring me in? Why?" She asked.

"You won't understand, but I'll try to explain it to you anyway. I owe you that much Alex." I answered. "It's true that we loved each other once and I probably still love you now if I gave it any thought, but I'm a private detective… I know that probably doesn't me much to someone like you, but it's who I am, who I've always been. If I were to disappear with you now, things would be nice and cozy for a while, but everything I've worked for all my life would mean nothing. I know that most guys in my profession are supposed to be crooked and unethical, but I never have been, at least not when it counted. I've got a handful of friends in this business, and they've always trusted that I'll do the right thing in the end. That's what's kept me going. Can't you see that walking away now would betray any trust they've had me."

"What about me Nick? What about us?" She asked.

"What about us? What if I do love you and you love me? I'm taking you in just the same." I kept the gun leveled at her and close by my side. "Now jump back over that rail and we'll walk out of here together," I ordered. She smiled at me, then laughed a little.

"I guess I always knew it would end this way Nick," she admitted. "But part of me hoped it might be different." She took two steps backwards towards the wall of falling water, then looked across at me. "I do love you Nick... But I'm not coming back with you." She turned suddenly and nose-dived off the edge, disappearing into the wall of white water. I stood there motionless for a moment, still holding the gun on the empty tunnel. I swallowed hard and tucked the Berretta away under my shoulder. A tear ran down my face as I turned and walked away.

Twenty-Nine: Payment in Full

I rode the elevator back up top, then staggered outside to the overlook at Horseshoe falls. I leaned over the railing and looked down at the raging white water pounding away at the base of the falls. I watched the water for nearly twenty minutes, expecting to see Alex's body emerge somewhere below, but it never did. I scanned the base of the falls and then the rocks along the river bed for as far as I could see, but she never appeared. After nearly an hour of eye strain, I gave up and started back to the hotel.

As I walked back down through Queen Victoria Park, I saw a man seated on one of the park benches smoking a pipe and looking across at the American side. He was dressed in a tan sports jacket with white trousers and brown patent leather shoes. He had a yellow scarf wrapped around his thin neck, and his gray hair was combed back neatly on either side. I took a seat on the bench next to him, pulled out a smoke and lit it. The man barely took notice of me, and just kept his eyes on the passing river.

"How's it going Preston," I asked. The man turned to me, somewhat startled, not quite believing what his eyes were telling him.

"Why it's you Chambers," he stumbled on his words. "What a pleasant coincidence to run into you up in this neck of the woods." I took a drag on my smoke.

"I wouldn't call it coincidence," I replied.

"You wouldn't?" he said. "You're not up here on vacation then?" He asked.

"Nope," I answered stoically.

"Well, then business I suppose," he concluded.

"That's right," I replied. "A dead-beat client of mine tried to stiff me by leaving the country a week ago, so I came up here to collect my fee." I leaned in close and let him see the Beretta under my shoulder. A bead of sweat ran down his pale brow.

"Look here Chambers," he blustered. "I fully intended to pay you when I returned from holiday next week."

"That's why you cleaned your place out and covered all the furniture with sheets?" I questioned.

He took out a handkerchief and wiped his clammy brow, then tucked it away in his pocket.

"I'd be more than happy to write a check for you right now Chambers," he offered. "What was the exact amount for your services?" He asked as he pulled out an alligator skin wallet and fumbled inside for a personal check.

"It was three hundred, plus another two to cover my trip up here," I reported. "Let's call it an even five hundred, but you'll be paying me in cash Scott."

"I simply don't have five hundred dollars on me," he answered nervously.

"How much do you have on you?" I asked. He thumbed inside his wallet and pulled out a mixed assortment of bills.

"A little over two hundred in cash," he answered. "You can take this as a deposit and I'll write you a personal check for the difference Chambers," he suggested.

"That's no good Preston," I replied. "I'll need the whole five hundred in cash." I stood up and back-handed him across his face, then took his wallet from his hands. I opened it and looked inside. At first it seemed empty, other than a driver's license and a receipt from his hotel. I searched a little deeper and found twelve neatly folded fifty-dollar travelers checks in one of the side pockets. I pulled them out and his face sank.

"You've got six hundred dollars in travelers checks here Preston," I commented. I counted out six of them and tucked the rest back inside his wallet. "Get your pen out and start signing," I ordered as I tossed his wallet back on his lap. He reluctantly drew out a gold Cross pen from his jacket and began signing the checks.

When he was done, I took the checks along with the cash and put them away in my wallet.

"This concludes our business Mr. Scott, unless you do something to reopen the case," I stated.

"What could I possibly do to re-open the case Chambers," he replied arrogantly. I leaned down to him and whispered into his ear.

"Well… You might do something stupid like calling your travel agent and reporting these checks as stolen," I suggested. "Then I'd have to reopen the case and come and find you again… and I would find you Preston. Only then I wouldn't be looking for money. You'd pay with a beating from me and whatever the hospital charges you for their services." He nervously tucked his wallet away in his jacket, then stood up.

"Consider the case closed Mr. Chambers, and paid in full," he added. I nodded and walked off.

It was almost dinner time when I returned to my hotel room. I unlocked the door and stepped inside. Evelyn was lying on the bed reading a book. She glanced over the pages at me.

"Find her?" she asked. I paused for a moment.

"No," I replied shaking my head. "Let's go out for dinner tonight, and we can head back home tomorrow," I suggested.

"Really?" She asked.

"Yeah… I've had my fill of Niagara Falls," I said sitting down on the bed beside her. She leaned over and kissed me.

"I don't know Nick," she commented. "I think I'd like to come back here someday, maybe on a honeymoon."

"Hey, weren't you supposed to be on your honeymoon about this time?" I asked.

"Yes, but you know that I decided to call it off."

"Cold feet huh?" I questioned. She shook her head.

"Not really. I just made plans with the wrong guy," she explained before leaning in and kissing me again.

Shadow Over Providence

A Nicholas Chambers Mystery

By Christopher J. Dacey

About the Author

Christopher Dacey is an author living in Coventry, Rhode Island. Shadow Over Providence is the sixth Nicholas Chambers novel in a series.

Chris holds a Master's Degree from the University of Rhode Island and is an avid fan of pulp fiction novels and film noir. He lives in Coventry, R.I. with his three children and wife Suzanne.

Nicholas Chambers Mysteries

Nicholas Chambers is a hard boiled, wise cracking private investigator working in the streets of Providence during the 1940's. His cases bring him into the underbelly of the city as he solves mysteries while staying one short step ahead of the law. Murder and espionage become part of wartime life during the early 1940's, and Chambers does his part to see that justice is done, while protecting his client's interests

Book 1. Argentine Mist

It's October 1941. As a tropical storm hits the City of Providence, private investigator Nicholas Chambers finds himself caught up in the search for a missing woman and gets entangled with the Providence underworld and a secretive group operating along the Rhode Island coastline. A midnight trip to a secluded house along Warwick Neck ignites the case and plunges Chambers into a mystery that tests his abilities to the limit.

Book 2. Long Winter's Nap

With only five days until Christmas 1942, Shepard's Department Store Vice President James Burkhart hires Private Investigator Nicholas Chambers to look into the murky past of his future son-in-law. The mystery deepens when an eccentric art collector hires Chambers to purchase a rare Austrian clock at auction. A beautiful French woman and a mysterious group operating on the outskirts of Providence draw Chambers deeper into the mystery, and open his eyes to an imminent threat facing his way of life.

Book 3. Mystery at Oceancrest

Private Detective Nicholas Chambers is summoned to oceanfront estate of retired millionaire Eugene Campbell, where he is hired to investigate the death of his daughter Vera five years earlier. Chambers reluctantly takes on the case, which leads him into a seedy Chinatown underworld and culminates at Oceancrest, where a web of deception and betrayal spanning the course of two decades is finally revealed.

Book 4. The Secret of Isabella Meer

Private Detective Nicholas Chambers arrives in the Port of Providence and reluctantly boards the SS Santa Rosa on a simple assignment; Sail to the Netherlands aboard a luxury liner, pick up a female passenger and accompany her back to the states. Soon an elderly woman is found dead in her cabin, another is missing, and a secret adversary aboard the ship is working against Chambers as he tries to uncover the secret of Isabella Meer.

Book 5. Remembered Murder

Private Detective Nicholas Chambers receives a midnight telephone call and is summoned to St. Paul's Roman Catholic Church in Cranston, R.I. Greeted by his childhood friend Fr. Richard O'Rourke, he is taken to the church bell tower. What he is shown there plunges him into a decade old mystery, testing the limits of his detective skills, and opening his eyes to the forces of good and evil at work in the world.

Book 6. Shadow over Providence

When Nick's secretary is found brutally murdered in his office, he suddenly becomes the authority's number one suspect. He pledges to track down her killer, but must first prove his own innocence. Nothing is what it seems to be in this case, as Chambers faces his most formidable hidden adversary....

Nicholas Chambers Mystery Series